Hitmen
Triumph

SIGMUND BROUWER

Brought to you by:
The READ ON! Literacy Project

With Special Thanks to our Sponsors:
- SCHLUMBERGER -
- COOLREADING.COM -
- THE CALGARY HITMEN -

Schlumberger

Greetings to students in Calgary as well as schools throughout Alberta, the Northwest Territories, and many other locations across Canada. On behalf of thousands of Schlumberger employees and our partners, The Calgary Hitmen Hockey Team, we are pleased to extend to you the "Literacy for Life"Program for the eighth straight year.

As the world's leading supplier of technologies to the oil and gas industry, Schlumberger recognizes the importance of literacy towards securing a good education. Having a strong foundation in both reading and writing is essential for young people to have success in school, get a good job and secure a positive future. Whether you aspire to be a young hockey superstar or excel in some other worthy pursuit, more than ever before, young people must have a good education. The ability to read well is fundamental to being able to learn in a complex and challenging world.

Throughout the years, the Literacy for Life Program has focused on developing educational partnerships in hundreds of schools through which Schlumberger staff and Hitmen Hockey players have assisted local educators in helping young people achieve greater success. I am very pleased to say that in 2007-2008, we have added to our team, and as a result hundreds of additional schools and thousands more young people will be impacted by this initiative. Hockey

---

Hall of Fame member Bryan Trottier and other former NHL stars like Al Conroy and Paul Kruse have increased our ability to reach out and touch even more young lives in more communities.

This year we are delighted to extend Hitmen Triumph to you for your reading enjoyment. As you are aware, the Calgary Hitmen practice hard to be winners on the ice. We encourage you to read this book, and keep reading, as practice will continue to help you become a better reader for life. Don't forget to take your collector's edition book to the Calgary Hitmen home games to get the signatures of your favorite players and be sure to participate in all the various activities in our program. You could win a visit to your school by the Calgary Hitmen Hockey Players, an author visit and writing workshop by Sigmund Brouwer, or a host of hockey collectable prizes.

At Schlumberger, we believe having a solid foundation in reading and writing is necessary for young people to be successful in life and reach their dreams. On behalf of all Schlumberger employees, the Calgary Hitmen Hockey Club, and myself we hope you enjoy reading this book and participating in the program.

Derek Normore

President, Schlumberger Canada Limited

Roster

8	Bortis, Kyle	C
9	Galiardi, T.J.	LC
10	Golicic, Bostjan	LW
11	Schaber, Chase	C
12	Sonne, Brett	LC
14	McMillan, Carson	RW
15	Kozun, Brandon	RW
17	Duval, Ian	C
18	Rowinski, Brendan	C
19	Schultz, Ian	RW
21	Stepan, Martin	LW
22	Kalinski, Devon	LW
25	White, Ryan	C
29	Fox, Ryan	RW
2	Postma, Paul	D
3	Mercer, Dan	D
4	Plante, Alex	D
5	Mackenzie, Matt	D
6	Frere, Eric	D
7	Seabrook, Keith	D
26	Gillen, Ryan	D
27	Alzner, Karl	D
28	Stone, Michael	D
31	Jones, Martin	G
33	Spence, Dan	G

President & CEO: Ken King
General Manager / Head Coach: Kelly Kisio
Associate Head Coach: Dave Lowry
Assistant Coach: Joel Otto
Video / Assistant Coach: Brent Kisio
Goaltending Coach: Darcy Wakaluk
Head Scout: Brad Whelen
Travelling Scout: Dan Bonar
Athletic Therapist: Will McMillan
Athletic Trainer / Equipment Manager: Blair Niekamp

Player Profile

Name: Kyle Bortis

Position: Left Wing

Height: 5'11

Weight: 190 lbs

Birthday: Aug. 28, 1988

Hometown: Saskatoon, SK

Draft Status: Eligible 2008

Nickname: Borty, Borts

Favorite pre-game meal: Chicken Fettuccini Alfredo

First time on skates: 3 years old

Favorite band: The Boys

If you were not a hockey player you would be a: Full time golfer

Special talent: Impersonations

How did you pick your jersey number: It was given to me after the trade.

Player Profile

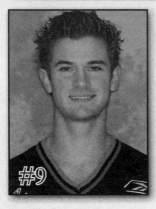

Name: TJ Galiardi
Position: Centre/Left Wing
Height: 6'1
Weight: 175 lbs
Birthday: Apr. 22, 1988
Hometown: Calgary, AB
Draft Status: Colorado Avalanche, Round 2, 2007

Nickname: Gally
Favorite pre-game meal: Pasta and Chicken
First time on skates: 4 years old
Favorite band: Damien Rice
If you were not a hockey player you would be a: squash player
Special talent: Good memory
How did you pick your jersey number: Best available

Player Profile

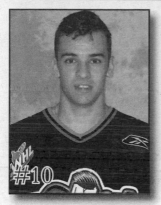

Name: Bostjan Golicic
Position: Left Wing
Height: 5'11
Weight: 187 lbs
Birthday: June 12, 1989
Hometown: Podbrezje, Slovenia
Draft Status: Eligible 2008

Nickname: Boss

Favorite pre-game meal: Tortellini (pasta)

First time on skates: 3.5 years

Favorite band: Chemical Brothers

If you were not a hockey player you would be a: House Music DJ

Special talent: Good at Darts

How did you pick your jersey number: I picked number 10 because Maradona, the best soccer player of all time, wore that number

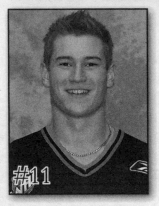

Name: Chase Schaber
Position: Centre
Height: 5'11
Weight: 183 lbs
Birthday: Jan. 3, 1991
Hometown: Red Deer, AB
Draft Status: Eligible 2009

Nickname: Shabes
First time on skates: 2 years old
Favorite band: Nickelback
If you were not a hockey player you would be a: Race car driver
Special talent: Unbelievably smart at Math
How did you pick your jersey number: It was an open number so I thought I would take 11 because I wore that number before.

Player Profile

Name: Brett Sonne

Position: Centre/Left Wing

Height: 6'0

Weight: 187 lbs

Birthday: May 16, 1989

Hometown: Maple Ridge, B.C.

Draft Status: St. Louis Blues, Round 3, 2007

Nickname: Sohnz

Favorite pre-game meal: Any pasta

First time on skates: Mom and Tots in Salmon Arm

If you were not a hockey player you would be a: Superhero

Special talent: Cooking

How did you pick your jersey number: It was given to me when I was 15.

Player Profile

Name: Carson McMillan

Position: Right Wing

Height: 6'2

Weight: 205 lbs

Birthday: Sept. 10, 1988

Hometown: Brandon, MB

Draft Status: Minnesota Wild, Round 7, 2007

Nickname: Macker

Favorite pre-game meal: Salmon and Rice

First time on skates: 3 years old

Favorite band: Alterbridge

If you were not a hockey player you would be a: Baseball player

Special talent: Stating movie quotes

How did you pick your jersey number: The best number left.

Player Profile

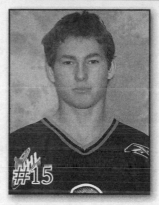

Name: Brandon Kozun
Position: Right Wing
Height: 5'8
Weight: 146 lbs
Birthday: Mar. 8, 1990
Hometown: Calgary, AB
Draft Status: Eligible 2008

Nickname: Kozy
Favorite pre-game meal: Depends on how I played in the previous game.
First time on skates: 2 years old
Favorite band: Rascal Flatts
If you were not a hockey player you would be a: All around jock
Special talent: Juggling
How did you pick your jersey number: When I was younger they didn't have my number so I picked 15 and it has stuck since.

Player Profile

Name: Ian Duval
Position: Centre/Left Wing
Height: 6'0
Weight: 202 lbs
Birthday: May 7, 1988
Hometown: Winnipeg, MB
Draft Status: Eligible 2008

Nickname: Duvy, Duv a loov
Favorite pre-game meal: Chicken Alfredo
First time on skates: 4 years old
Favorite band: The Boys
If you were not a hockey player you would be a: Golfer
Special talent: Belly Dancing
How did you pick your jersey number: Best one available

Player Profile

Name: Brendan Rowinski

Position: Center

Height: 5'11

Weight: 185 lbs

Birthday: Jan. 9, 1990

Hometown: Winnipeg, MB

Draft Status: Eligible 2008

Nickname: Row Daddy, Row, Row Diggity, Row Diggity Dog

Favorite pre-game meal: Spaghetti and Meat Sauce

First time on skates: 1 year old

Favorite band: Guns N' Roses

If you were not a hockey player you would be a: The arch nemesis of Jonsey and his sidekick Gilley

Special talent: My hair turns into rope and ties people up

How did you pick your jersey number: There were only a few left and I like 18.

Player Profile

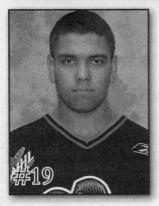

Name: Ian Schultz
Position: Right Wing
Height: 6'2
Weight: 182 lbs
Birthday: Feb. 4, 1990
Hometown: Calgary, AB
Draft Status: Eligible 2008

Nickname: Schultzy

Favorite pre-game meal: Steak and Pasta

First time on skates: 3 years old

Favorite band: 50 Cent, T.I.P.

If you were not a hockey player you would be a:
Football player

Special talent: I can say the alphabet backwards

How did you pick your jersey number: Looks good on me.

Player Profile

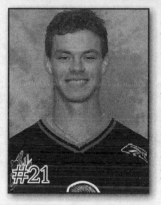

Name: Martin Stepan
Position: Left Wing
Height: 5'10
Weight: 172 lbs
Birthday: Mar. 18, 1989
Hometown: Skalica, Slovakia
Draft Status: Eligible 2008

Nickname: Steps

Favorite pre-game meal: Chicken and Rice

First time on skates: 2 1/2 years old

Favorite band: Krystof, Metallica, Red Hot Chili Peppers

If you were not a hockey player you would be a: Psychologist

Special talent: Speaks four languages

How did you pick your jersey number: I like 21.

Player Profile

Name: Devon Kalinski
Position: Centre/Left Wing
Height: 5'11
Weight: 185 lbs
Birthday: Jan. 1, 1990
Hometown: La Corey, AB
Draft Status: Eligible 2008

Nickname: Killer

Favorite pre-game meal: Cereal

First time on skates: 3 years old on the dug out

Favorite band: Tim McGraw

If you were not a hockey player you would be a:
Pro Wrestler

Special talent: Thumb Wrestling

How did you pick your jersey number: Looked
fast.

Player Profile

Name: Ryan White
Position: Centre
Height: 6'0
Weight: 213 lbs
Birthday: Mar. 17, 1988
Hometown: Brandon, MB
Draft Status: Montreal Canadiens, Round 3, 2006

Nickname: Whitey

Favorite pre-game meal: Quiznos

First time on skates: 3 years old

Favorite band: The Boys

If you were not a hockey player you would be a: Rock Star

Special talent: Telling stories

How did you pick your jersey number: It was given to me.

Player Profile

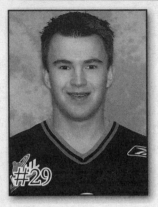

Name: Ryan Fox
Position: Right Wing
Height: 6'0
Weight: 187 lbs
Birthday: April 26, 1990
Hometown: Creighton, SK
Draft Status: Eligible 2008

Nickname: Foxy
Favorite pre-game meal: Chicken Fettucini Alfredo
First time on skates: 5 years old
Favorite band: Silverstein, Bullet for my Valentine
If you were not a hockey player you would be a: undecided
Special talent: Guitar Hero
How did you pick your jersey number: #9 was taken

Player Profile

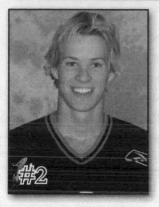

Name: Paul Postma

Position: Defence

Height: 6'3

Weight: 182 lbs

Birthday: Feb. 22, 1989

Hometown: Red Deer, AB

Draft Status: Atlanta Thrashers, Round 7, 2007

Nickname: Posty, Eddy

Favorite pre-game meal: Chicken Tortellini

First time on skates: 2 years old

Favorite band: All American Rejects

If you were not a hockey player you would be a: Scuba diving instructor in Hawaii

Special talent: Making friends

How did you pick your jersey number: It was given to me.

Player Profile

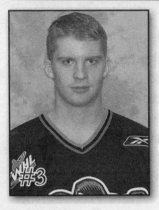

Name: Dan Mercer

Position: Defence

Height: 6'3

Weight: 205 lbs

Birthday: May 4, 1987

Hometown: West Vancouver, BC

Draft Status: Free Agent

Nickname: Merce, Murr

Favorite pre-game meal: Tortellini

First time on skates: 5 years old

Favorite band: The Beatles

If you were not a hockey player you would be a: Stock Broker

Special talent: Calling bluffs

How did you pick your jersey number: By default.

Player Profile

Name: Alex Plante
Position: Defence
Height: 6'5
Weight: 212 lbs
Birthday: May 9, 1989
Hometown: Brandon, MB
Draft Status: Edmonton Oilers, Round 1, 2007

Nickname: Planter
Favorite pre-game meal: Spaghetti and Vegetables
First time on skates: 7 years old
Favorite band: Buck Cherry
If you were not a hockey player you would be a: No clue
Special talent: Skipping stones
How did you pick your jersey number: It was my father's number.

Player Profile

Name: Matt Mackenzie
Position: Defence
Height: 6'1
Weight: 185 lbs
Birthday: Oct. 15, 1991
Hometown: New Westminster, BC
Draft Status: Eligible 2010

Nickname: Walt
Favorite pre-game meal: Pasta and Chicken
First time on skates: 3 years old
Favorite band: Nickelback
If you were not a hockey player you would be a: Volleyball Player
How did you pick your jersey number: Best available.

Player Profile

Name: Eric Frere
Position: Defence
Height: 6'2
Weight: 188 lbs
Birthday: Nov. 15, 1988
Hometown: Trochu, AB
Draft Status: Eligible 2008

Nickname: Frerezy

Favorite pre-game meal: Chicken and Rice

First time on skates: 4 years old on the 4 blade skates

Favorite band: Rise Against, AFI, Toby Keith

If you were not a hockey player you would be a: Business owner

Special talent: Movie quotes

How did you pick your jersey number: Had it back in Atom.

Player Profile

Name: Keith Seabrook
Position: Defence
Height: 6'0
Weight: 200 lbs
Birthday: Aug. 2, 1988
Hometown: Delta, BC
Draft Status: Washington Capitals, Round 2, 2006

Nickname: Seabs
Favorite pre-game meal: Chicken and Rice/Pasta
First time on skates: 3 years old
Favorite band: Atreyu
If you were not a hockey player you would be a: Professional Ping Pong Player
Special talent: I can run really fast
How did you pick your jersey number: Seven looks good on me.

Player Profile

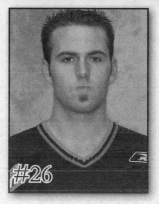

Name: Ryan Gillen

Position: Defence/Forward, Rover

Height: 6'6

Weight: 235 lbs

Birthday: May 1, 1987

Hometown: Golden, BC

Draft Status: Free Agent

Nickname: Gilley, Dad, Big Horse, Big Pappi

Favorite pre-game meal: Pasta and Chicken

First time on skates: 3 years old

Favorite band: Audioslave, Red Hot Chili Peppers

If you were not a hockey player you would be a: Jone's Sidekick

Special talent: Growing a beard very quickly

How did you pick your jersey number: Five wasn't available.

Player Profile

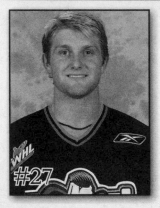

Name: Karl Alzner

Position: Defence

Height: 6'2

Weight: 209 lbs

Birthday: Sept. 24, 1988

Hometown: Burnaby, BC

Draft Status: Washington Capitals, Round 1, 2007

Nickname: Karl

Favorite pre-game meal: Pasta and Tuna

First time on skates: 2 years old

Favorite band: Nickelback

If you were not a hockey player you would be a: Sports Analyst

Special talent: I can touch my nose with my tongue.

How did you pick your jersey number: Scott Niedermayer

Player Profile

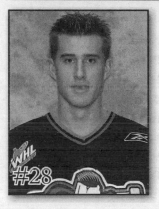

Name: Michael Stone

Position: Defence

Height: 6'3

Weight: 206 lbs

Birthday: June 7, 1990

Hometown: Winnipeg, MB

Draft Status: Eligible 2008

Nickname: Stoner

Favorite pre-game meal: Penne Alfredo

First time on skates: 3 years old

Favorite band: Tim McGraw

If you were not a hockey player you would be a: Businessman

Special talent: Good impression of a bobblehead.

How did you pick your jersey number: Best one left.

Player Profile

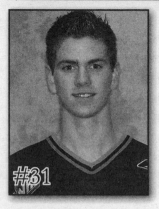

Name: Martin Jones

Position: Goaltender

Height: 6'3

Weight: 178 lbs

Birthday: Jan. 10, 1990

Hometown: North Vancouver, BC

Draft Status: Eligible 2008

Nickname: Jonesy

Favorite pre-game meal: Tortellini Alfredo

First time on skates: 3 years old

Favorite band: Keith Urban, Kenny Chesney

If you were not a hockey player you would be a: Superhero

Special talent: Shoot spaghetti out of my fingers

How did you pick your jersey number: 31 was my minor hockey number.

Player Profile

Name: Dan Spence
Position: Goaltender
Height: 6'0
Weight: 181 lbs
Birthday: Jan. 17, 1988
Hometown: Langley, BC
Draft Status: Eligible 2008

Nickname: Spencey
Favorite pre-game meal: Pasta
First time on skates: 8 years old
Favorite band: Nickelback
If you were not a hockey player you would be a:
Football Player
Special talent: Driving fast
How did you pick your jersey number: It was given to me.

Hitmen Triumph

 One

I stood in the dark on the first tee box at a country club so expensive I couldn't afford to work there as a dishwasher. I had a driver in my hand, ready to hit a golf ball down the fairway. If I hit the ball anywhere but straight, it would cost me twenty-five hundred dollars.

Earlier that day, I had golfed the same hole during a charity golf tournament for the Calgary Hitmen hockey team. So I knew how difficult it was. Water on both sides. Trees in the worst places. That was during the day—and I'd taken two shots, plus two penalty strokes for going into the water, just to get the ball on the green. Then three more putts to drop it in the hole. A big fat seven on the scorecard.

Now it was night. As in dark sky, bright

1

stars, a crescent moon and the outlines of trees around me. As in no sunlight to help me see the ball on the little white tee. No sunlight to see where the ball went after I hit it.

My twin brother, Nathan, stood across from me, pointing the beam of a flashlight at the ball he had just handed me. Nate had drawn a circle around the Nike swoosh using a blue felt marker. There would be no mistaking that it was my ball. If we found it after I hit it. Otherwise twenty-five hundred dollars were gone. It had been a very stupid bet.

A tiny beetle crawled across the top of the ball. My focus was so strong that I saw the bug's shadow etched across the white of the golf ball.

There were probably a hundred other people around the tee box to watch me hit the ball. Among them was a girl named Mercedes. Most of them—except for Mercedes—were hoping Nate and I would lose our bet.

The center of the green was 514 yards away. If I took four shots or less to get the ball in the hole, we would win. If I took five strokes—which was par on this hole—nobody would win, and nobody would lose. But if I took more than five shots, the way I had earlier in the day, we would lose. A lot. I had bet a thousand dollars. Nate had put another fifteen hundred on me.

Yeah. Twenty-five hundred dollars.

Nate and I were seventeen and played on the same line for the Calgary Hitmen. Maybe someday we'd make it to the next level, into the NHL, where players could afford to lose that kind of cash. But even after working all summer, we didn't have that much money saved up between the two of us. Not only that, I wondered if we would both get suspended before the first exhibition game of the season if our coach found out about this stunt.

"Rip it, Radar," Nate said. My name is Nolan, but I've been called Radar since I was a kid.

If Nate was nervous, there was no way to tell. He held the flashlight steady. He should have been nervous though. I could hit the ball far, but I didn't always hit it straight.

I knew I'd have to swing soon. Just not yet. The beetle had moved to the side of the ball, where my clubface would mash into it. It wasn't right, killing it for no reason. The bug was just out for a walk. It had no idea that I was in the middle of something very stupid.

"The kid's chicken!" someone in the crowd yelled. "He can't pull the trigger!"

Others laughed with him.

I ignored them. I squatted down and gently blew the beetle off the ball.

"Get it going!" someone else yelled. "We don't have all night!"

I heard the laughter as I stood again, but not the way most people hear it. The best way to describe it is that it sounded as if it was coming through water, but that's not really an accurate description either. I have progressive hearing loss. If I hadn't had an operation to attach electrodes inside my skull to a piece of equipment on my ear, I wouldn't be able to hear.

"Do it, Radar," Nate said. "Rip it long and straight."

Easy for him to say. He wasn't the one holding the driver. Staring at a white ball. Hoping to hit it at least 275 yards. Down a fairway. Between water. At night. With twenty-five hundred dollars on the line.

I lifted the club away from the ball and turned into my backswing.

With one thought.

Nolan, at breakfast you must have had an extra bowl of stupid.

Two

When a guy does something stupid, chances are, one way or another, it's because of a girl. In this case, it was two girls. So I guess that's why I had done something doubly stupid.

One of the girls was Sheila. The Calgary Hitmen golf tournament had been held to raise money for the Special Olympics. Sheila was a runner who competed in the Special Olympics. She was about my age, but because she had Down syndrome, she had the sweetness and innocence of a six-year-old.

After the tournament, all the golfers had gone to a banquet at the fancy clubhouse. Sheila was one of the Special Olympics athletes who had been invited to the banquet to meet the golfers who were donating money to the cause.

She had stopped by our table, where two teams of golfers sat. Like at most charity tournaments, there were five golfers on each team—one Calgary Hitmen player plus four golfers who each paid a big entry fee to help the charity.

Sheila had almond-shaped eyes and short brown hair that made her wide face seem even more innocent. She wore a pretty yellow dress, and I could tell she felt very grown up and excited to be at the tournament. She had talked with all ten of us at the table for a few minutes before she moved on to the next table.

For me, the trouble started as she left, when one of the businessmen on our team started talking the way Sheila talked. A little slower. And he talked through his nose. Then he laughed.

I might have let it go, except Sheila heard him. She hadn't quite reached the other table. She stopped and looked back at him. Tears started to trickle down her cheeks.

"Sir," I said to the guy. Bob Jones. He owned a car dealership and had made sure everybody knew about it. He was in his forties. Loud golf shirt. Loud sunburn. Loud voice. "That was wrong."

Like Sheila, I spoke in a way that wasn't quite normal. Because I began losing my hearing when I was little, words don't quite come out the same as they do for most people.

"Sir," Bob Jones said in slow weird way. "That was wrong."

He laughed the way he had laughed after mocking Sheila.

He was trying to bully me into silence. I hate bullies. There is only one way to deal with them. Head on.

"Wow," I said. "You are very funny."

He mocked me again, imitating the way I speak, adding more nasal sounds. "Wow. You are very funny."

He laughed again. His buddies laughed, but only a little. Like he was embarrassing them by mocking the way I speak.

Words come out the way I hear them. When I was in grades one and two, kids had teased me a lot about the way I talk. In grade three, I had a teacher who spoke to me about it when I was crying in the corner of the classroom after a bully had picked on me. She said that I couldn't control what other people did. That I could only control what I decided to do about it. She said I could choose to try to hide the way I spoke. Or that I could choose to accept who I was and never be ashamed of it and never let that stop me from speaking. She said I could spend my life running away. Or I could spend my life fighting back and showing people what

7

I was capable of doing. When I discovered how much I loved hockey, the choice became a lot easier. I decided to show people what I could do. Especially bullies.

"Brilliant," I said to the car dealership guy. After grade three, I learned that the best defense against bullies was to stand up to them. "Stick with the easy targets like a Special Olympics athlete and a deaf guy who has trouble pronouncing words. What's next, shooting birds while they are still in the nest? Or do you prefer to break the eggs before they hatch to make sure you absolutely can't miss?"

The table became quiet.

"Do you know who you are talking to?" he said. His sunburned face got even redder.

"If it was multiple choice, I'd have to guess a) an idiot, b) a jerk, c) a butthead or d) all of the above. Want to try repeating that the way I speak? Or is your brain too little to remember such a long sentence?"

Jones leaned forward. "Don't push me. I'm already in a bad enough mood because of all the bets I lost today. If you had hit even one decent shot during the tournament, our team would have finished in the top three today. You've got radar, all right. For finding trouble with your golf shots."

"I don't play golf for the Hitmen," I said. "I

play hockey. That's a game played on the ice. With a stick and a puck and skates. Betting on my golfing ability is as smart as licking a flagpole when it's minus twenty. But you don't strike me as that smart."

Jones half stood. "Do you have any idea how much money I donate to this event?"

"Because you care so much for the Special Olympics athletes? Or because it makes you look good and gives you a big tax write-off?"

Jones pushed back his chair and stood up all the way, as if he expected that would scare me.

I stood too. Did I mention I hate bullies?

So far, the argument had not gone beyond our table. It wouldn't, as long as the guy didn't swing at me. But if he did, I was ready. I will not let bullies push me around.

That's when the other girl stepped between us.

Mercedes.

She was not a Special Olympics athlete. She was a tournament volunteer who had handed out bottles of water to the golfers at one of the holes. She was tall like me. About my age too. Long, burnished copper hair. Freckles. With a very, very nice smile. She had talked to me on the golf course, and I knew she was called Mercedes because of her name tag. I would never have asked. I have no problem facing bullies, but pretty girls terrify me.

"Gentlemen," she said, "how about we sit down before this gets crazy?"

"Gentlemen don't make fun of Special Olympics athletes," I said. "Sheila is crying because she heard him. Maybe Mr. Jones should go over and apologize before he sits down."

Her eyes narrowed as she stared at Jones and spoke to me. "In that case, Nolan, make sure your first punch is a good one."

"Hey, smart mouth," Jones said to me. "How's this? I'm going to rip up the thousand-dollar check I had in my pocket ready to donate. That will make up for the bets I lost today because of you. Two balls in the water on the first hole. I should have known you were a loser."

"Next time," I said, "I'll enjoy who I golf with, and I'll hit the fairway."

"As if you could," he said.

"No problem," I said.

His snarl became a smile. Like he was a cat discovering a crippled mouse. "Really? Care to put your money where your mouth is?"

Conversations at the other tables had stopped. Everyone was watching us.

Mercedes tugged on my sleeve. I was wearing my Hitmen jersey. Number seventeen.

"Don't fall for it," she whispered. "Just sit

down."

I made the mistake of looking into her brown eyes. They were as beautiful as her smile. I also made the mistake of looking over at Sheila. Her shoulders were hunched. She was still crying.

"Tell you what," I said to Jones. I didn't know how I was going to do it, but I would find a way. "Any time you want, I'll play that hole and prove it."

"Really," he said. His eyes gleamed. "How about for the thousand dollars? As soon as the banquet is finished?"

This guy was a bully. I knew what he was trying to do. Shove me around using money instead of muscles. He had a lot of money. I didn't. He thought it would make me back down. He didn't know I hate bullies so much I was not going to let him do it, even if it cost me a thousand dollars I didn't have.

"Sure," I said. "I'll put a thousand dollars on it."

That's when I knew I had eaten an extra bowl of stupid for breakfast.

 # Three

On the tee box, my club came down and made solid contact with the golf ball. It had that satisfying feel of ripping a great slap shot.

I can pound slap shots. And golf balls. In hockey, the slap shot usually goes where I want it to go. In golf, not so often.

The golf ball instantly disappeared into the black of night. I sure hoped it had gone straight. I wondered if there would be a splash. Not that I'd really be able to hear it that well. But my implant did bring me most sounds, even if the sounds weren't very clear.

"Yeah, buddy!" my brother Nate yelled. "You go, Radar!"

He whistled and cheered. If there had been a

splash, there was no way to tell above the noise he was making.

Had the ball landed on the fairway?

Only one way to find out. Walk and look. And hope.

Nate led the way with his flashlight. I followed close behind. The rest of the crowd stayed with us.

"Nate," I said in a low voice, "this is crazy. Why did you bet another fifteen hundred dollars? You can't afford to lose it."

"Got twenty C-notes in my wallet," he said. "That will cover it."

"C-notes?"

"Hundred dollar bills," he said. "Cash takes up less room if you keep hundreds instead of twenties."

I walked a few steps down the grass of the fairway as what he had said sank into my mind. Nate had two thousand dollars cash?

"Did you rob a bank?" I asked, only half joking.

"Didn't need to," he answered. He flicked his flashlight back and forth across the fairway. "While you were playing for the Warriors, I learned a thing or two about making money."

I thought about it, but kept my questions to myself. I'd spent my first season in the WHL on the Moosejaw Warriors while Nate had played his rookie year in Calgary for the Hitmen. I wondered what else he'd been doing during the hockey season to make that kind of cash.

Right now though, I had something more important to worry about: making sure I didn't lose a thousand dollars of my own.

"Hey!" Nate said. "Look!"

His flashlight beam found a golf ball, sitting nicely on top of the mowed grass.

"Are you sure the ball is his?" came a voice from the crowd. Bob Jones, Mr. Car Dealer.

Nate walked closer. The flashlight beam clearly showed the Nike swoosh and a blue circle around it.

"Mine," I said. One shot down without going into the water. But could I hit another one straight enough to stay dry?

I pulled a fairway wood from my bag.

"What are you doing?" Nate asked.

"I saw the yardage to the green on a sprinkler head," I answered. "I think I can get on the green from here. If I miss and go in the water, I'll still have a chance at a par if I can get it up and down after taking my penalty stroke."

"No," he said, "play it safe. Hit two shots from here to get on the green. Then you'll have two putts to knock it in the hole to make par."

"I'm not a good putter," I said. "If I can knock it on the green with this shot, I can take three putts for a five."

"No," he said, "play it safe."

"No," I said, "all I need is one straight shot."

Nate put his hand on my shoulder. "I've got another thousand in the car. Do it my way, and I'll cover your bet if you lose."

He had another thousand dollars?

"The kid will never hit the green from here," Bob Jones said. "He's too afraid."

Yes, I was afraid. But I guessed Jones was trying to get me to go for the green. And if that's what he wanted, it was exactly what I didn't want.

"I'll play it safe," I told Nate.

So I took a shorter club from my bag. I stood over the ball. I swallowed to try to get some moisture in my dry mouth. I took another swing. Again, the ball disappeared into the darkness.

Would this one hit water?

"Go, buddy!" Nate yelled. "Yahoo! You show 'em! Radar! That's my boy!"

Again, with all the noise he made, nobody was able to hear if my ball splashed.

Again, all I could do was walk and look. And hope.

Less than a minute later, we found the ball in the center of the fairway. Right beside a sprinkler head that showed it was only a hundred yards to the green.

15

The crowd was buzzing. To me, the words weren't clear; it truly did sound like buzzing.

"Great shot," Nate said. "Think you can hit the green from here?"

"Going to have to," I said.

Nate yelled at Bob Jones, "Hey, buddy, I got another five hundred that says he'll hit the ball closer to the hole than you can from here. Want to take the bet and try a shot after he hits his?"

Nate shone the flashlight on Bob Jones's face. Bob put up his hand to shield his eyes. It got very quiet as everyone waited for his answer.

"Nah," Jones finally said. "I'm already going to take enough of your money."

People around him laughed.

"Nice try," someone hollered. "Now who's a chicken?"

"Just hit the ball," Jones snapped.

So I did.

 Four

It was a terrible swing. It didn't feel right. As if I had hit the ball off the toe of the clubface instead of square in the center.

"Go, buddy!" Nate yelled, slapping my back. "Great swing, Radar! You got him now! Yahoo!"

I didn't feel as excited. I was sure, by the way it felt, that I'd knocked the ball into the water by the green. I should have known something was wrong, but I was too worried to think about it.

Nate marched forward to the green. We all followed, like he was the Pied Piper.

And sure enough, six feet from the pin was my Nike golf ball, with the blue circle around the

17

swoosh. Somehow, my bad swing had worked.

Nate slapped my back again.

There was applause from the crowd. I gave a fist pump. I'd hit three shots to get there. If I sank the putt for a birdie, I'd win. If I missed from that close, all I would have to do was tap it in for a par and a tie. Things were looking good.

Until Mercedes joined me and Nate at my golf bag.

"Hey," Mercedes said to me softly. "I found your golf ball."

"What?" I said just as quietly. "It's right there. On the green."

"I have one in my pocket that looks just like it," she whispered. "A blue circle around the Nike swoosh. You better hope no one finds another one too."

"Please," Nate said to Mercedes. "Keep it to yourself. I'll give you half the money."

I finally understood what had happened. I understood why Nate had yelled every time I'd hit the ball so that no one could hear if it splashed. Why he'd told me to play a shorter club instead of going for the green in two. Why the ball that I thought I'd hit off the toe of my club had landed so close to the hole instead of dropping into the water beside the green.

"Give me the ball," I said to Mercedes. If Nate had been setting this up to rip people off,

I wasn't going to let him do it. "Trust me on this."

She dug it out of her pocket and handed it to me. I grabbed the putter and marched toward the ball on the green.

I was mad. Very mad.

So mad that I knew I was going to sink the putt.

Nate shone the flashlight on the ball. I didn't take any time over it. The ball clicked off the face of my putter and rolled into the center of the cup. Four strokes—birdie. We had won the bet. All twenty-five hundred dollars.

Everybody roared.

I put up my hand to silence them.

"Guys," I said. "It was fun tricking all of you."

The quiet got even quieter, if that was possible. A few frogs croaked from the pond to break that silence.

"Nobody has to pay out their bets," I said. "But in the spirit of the fun we just had, Nate and I would like to ask you to donate half of what you would have lost to the Special Olympics."

I turned to Nate. "Isn't that right, Nate?"

He was smiling through gritted teeth and spoke so that only I could hear him. "Nolan,

I set this up for a good reason. Just let me explain."

Sure. Explain that he wanted to steal. All along, I'd thought he was trying to protect me.

"So," I said to the crowd, "if we can make you laugh about this, how many of you want to donate instead of paying out?"

"What's the deal?" someone in the crowd yelled out.

I reached into the cup and pulled out the ball. Then I took the ball that Mercedes had found. I held both of them out for people to see.

"Matching golf balls," I said. I knew my words sounded funny to them, but I'd long ago decided not to let that stop me. "While we were still in the clubhouse, my brother ran out ahead and planted matching golf balls on the fairway and on the green. Then he ran back to meet me on the tee-box and hold the flashlight for me. All I had to do was hit a shot, then go to the next ball and hit another shot. Same with the third shot. All along there was a ball on the green, right by the pin, waiting for me to get there."

It took a few seconds for people to understand. Then they started laughing.

Bob Jones stomped up to me, and the laughter stopped.

"You cheated," he said to me. "You didn't

win the bet. You owe me a thousand dollars."

"Everybody thinks it's funny that we fooled you," I said quietly. "Want to look like a sore loser? But if everybody sees you shake my hand and you put that thousand dollars back into the charity, they'll think you're a good guy and talk about it for years. How much is that worth in advertising?"

Jones took a deep breath. Then he smiled. I could see it hurt him to put that smile on his face.

He turned around and faced the crowd.

"I'm in for donating my bet to the Special Olympics," he said loudly. He put his arm around my shoulder while he spoke. Like we were best of friends. "Let's have another big round of applause for these two smart young men and the entertainment they gave us to-night."

Five

Some people like the fall when it looks like a postcard. Trees with brilliant orange and red leaves. Blue sky in the background. No clouds. No wind.

Me, I hate the postcard look. It was on a day like that in grade five when I was called to the principal's office. I got there ahead of Nate, who was in the other grade five classroom. All through school, they put us in different classrooms. Easier on the teachers. The only way to tell us apart back then was the way I speak. I don't hear clearly and I speak slowly, like someone who's learning a foreign language.

The minister of our church was waiting for us on that postcard-perfect fall day. He was tall and bald and had a serious look on his face. Our principal, a short woman with gray hair, didn't know where to look and kept rubbing her hands together. Even before Nate got there, I could tell something was wrong. My hearing is bad, not my brain.

On that beautiful fall day, when Nate finally arrived in the principal's office, the minister spoke slowly and told us that a big truck had gone through a stop sign and crashed into our car just as our mother and father were driving through the intersection.

The minister had talked to us as if we were five years old, not boys in grade five. He had tried to make us feel better by telling us our parents would not have felt any pain when the cement truck hit them. He told us that they had gone to a better place. Nate didn't—or wouldn't—understand. I had walked out of the office and out of the school and down the street underneath trees with brilliant orange and red leaves, looking up at the clear blue sky and trying not to think about anything. I walked for five miles. I slept under a bridge that night. I didn't go home for a day. When I got back, it wasn't home anyway. Not without Mom and Dad. I didn't care that the cops had been looking for me for twenty-four hours.

So you can understand why beautiful fall

days put me in a bad mood.

It was that kind of day when I walked through the parking lot from my car—an old green Toyota Camry—to the Saddledome for our first game of the season, against the Red Deer Rebels.

A month had passed since the charity golf tournament. Before the tournament, pre-season had gone well. Exhibition games too. I was left winger on the line with Nate, and he was center. He'd scored a bunch of goals, and I'd had plenty of assists. We're twins. I can't explain how, but I know where he's going before he gets there. It was almost like passing to myself—except I rarely got passes back. Nate liked scoring goals. I liked winning games. I didn't need the spotlight. He did.

After the charity golf tournament though, things had not been too good. When it came to Nate, my radar had vanished. Thinking about it put me in a bad mood.

Just like the postcard view. Behind me was the Calgary skyline against the blue sky. All the tall buildings. The Calgary Tower with the revolving restaurant. Yup, another postcard view. If you liked postcard views.

As I walked, I kept my eye on the Saddledome so that I wouldn't have to see a beautiful fall sky or the trees with orange and red leaves. Players arrived long before the game started, so there weren't many people there yet. The parking lot was almost empty.

Two guys in a new red Mustang drove into the parking lot. Both wore ball caps and sunglasses. I knew this because the driver sped toward me like he was going to run me over. I stared into the car's grill and windshield until he swerved the car sideways and stopped right beside me.

The driver grinned. He was a few years older than me. He had long blond hair. The passenger was about the same age, but he had dark hair that wasn't quite as long. They were big guys. Really big. Like they worked out and used steroids.

The driver leaned his arm out the window. He was wearing a black T-shirt. The sleeve had moved up his arm, and I saw the tattoo of an eagle.

"Nate," the driver said.

It wasn't the first time that I had been mistaken for Nate. It happened less these days, because I worked out and I had more bulk than Nate did. The extra muscles helped, going into the corners to fight for the puck. I was wearing a loose sweater though, and the driver probably couldn't tell that I weighed twenty pounds more than Nate.

I should have told him I was Nolan. But the driver was holding a plain white envelope out to me. In the month since the charity tournament, I'd spent a lot of time wondering about the cash that Nate had used for betting. I confess that was on my mind as I saw the envelope.

"Here you are, dude," the driver said, holding out the envelope. "Play a good game tonight. Don't get hurt. We'll see you tomorrow night. Usual time. Usual place."

I still didn't say anything. I took the envelope.

Yes, it was dishonest. I won't pretend anything else. I won't make excuses. It was wrong. I did it. I took the envelope that he thought was going to Nate.

I nodded. Speaking would have let the driver know I wasn't Nate. Nate wasn't deaf.

The driver grinned. Gave a thumbs-up. Then he burned rubber as he blasted out of the parking lot in the shiny red Mustang. Nice car. Expensive car.

I opened the envelope. Nate's envelope.

It held one-hundred dollar bills. Ten of them. Clean, crisp and new.

 # Six

I found Nate in the dressing room with a few other players who had arrived early. When I stopped beside him, no one paid much attention to the two of us. A few other guys were already there. Some of them were sitting and rolling tape onto the blades of their sticks. Others were talking quietly, telling jokes.

"Here, Nate," I said, handing him the envelope. "Some guys just gave this to me. They must have gotten you and me mixed up."

This was about as much as I had said to him since the night of the charity golf tournament. After it ended, he'd found me at my car. Our argument had been short, and I remembered every word.

"If Mercedes hadn't found that other ball, would you have even told me what was happening? Or just taken the money? And what about all that extra cash in your pocket? What's happening, Nate? Why are you keeping secrets from me?"

"I can't tell you," he had answered. "Trust me, okay?"

"Why don't you trust me and tell me what's happening?"

"When I can, I will," he had said.

"Then I guess we don't have anything to talk about until then."

I was mad and I had walked away. I shouldn't have. Now there was a big wall between us; it was going to stay there until he trusted me enough to tell me what was happening.

If it hadn't been for the fact that we played on the same hockey team, I'm sure we wouldn't have even seen each other again.

Now Nate took the envelope.

"Did you look in it?" Nate asked. His voice was cold.

"No." It was a lie. I was hoping he would tell me about the money in the envelope without me asking. Or finally tell me how he got all the money he was able to gamble at the charity golf tournament. Maybe then I could start trusting him again. Large amounts of cash delivered in plain white envelopes are very suspicious.

"Next time," Nate said, "open your mouth a little earlier and say something. That way there won't be any confusion."

Had he just insulted the way I speak? Or did he mean I should have told them my name?

"Whatever," I said.

He folded the envelope and put it in his front pocket. He stared at me. I stared back. The night of the charity golf tournament was a big wall between us that both of us pretended wasn't there.

Who knows how long we might have stared at each other. Fortunately, another player stepped into the dressing room and told us to stop blocking traffic.

Nate moved toward his equipment. I sat down by mine.

I dressed for the game in total silence. The silence of not speaking. The silence of being deaf. The silence of feeling like I no longer had a brother.

 # Seven

Three to three against the Rebels. Four minutes, ten seconds left in the game. I was in the players' box, watching, as a Rebels forward got dinged two minutes for tripping. That gave us a one-man advantage on the upcoming power play.

The crowd was roaring for the Hitmen. I knew that because I could see the hands clapping and the mouths moving. But I couldn't hear it. My world was total silence. When I play hockey, I don't wear the processor that delivers audio signals to the implant in my skull. I don't wear the magnetic "spider" on my skull either. The spider is a flat circular device a bit bigger than a quarter. It is connected to the processor on my ear by a thin wire hidden by my hair. The equipment is too expensive and, on the ice, too easy to break.

I felt a tap on my shoulder. Jonathan Koch, our coach. Everyone just called him Coach Jon. He was in his early thirties, wide and strong, with dark hair. He could bench press three hundred pounds. We never messed with him.

He held up a small whiteboard. He'd written out instructions for me. Coach Jon did that because he didn't trust that I would always be able to read his lips and understand every word.

Some people who have been deaf for a long time before getting cochlear implants learn sign language and lip-reading. I knew many of them called themselves "deafies" and were proud of how well they coped with their hearing loss.

Others, like me, received implants when we lost our hearing as children. We learned to understand sounds through the implants. We weren't forced to read lips or use sign language. Still, I was good at it. Good but not great.

But all of us with hearing loss become very good at understanding the world by watching it. Deaf drivers are usually much better than hearing drivers because they concentrate on what appears in front of the car, not what's on the stereo. I know it made me a better hockey player—everyone said it seemed like I saw everything that happened around me. Off the ice, I'd always concentrated on people's faces as they spoke, and I could read lips.

Coach Jon didn't speak to me. He just held up the whiteboard with instructions: *RADAR, MAKE SURE YOU DON'T GIVE AWAY THE PUCK*!

I nodded. I knew what he meant. For the whole game, my passes from the left side to Nate at center had been off target.

As the other guys on the line shift went onto the ice, Coach Jon wiped the words off the board. He quickly wrote something else down.

GO GET THEM!

He smiled and patted my back. I stepped onto the ice to join my teammates.

We lined up in the Rebels' zone, with the linesman dropping the puck in the circle to the left of the Rebels' goalie. As left winger, instead of staying on the boards, I took a position above the circle, directly behind Nate, who stepped in to take the draw.

The linesman snapped his hand down as he dropped the puck. Nate fought for it but lost the draw. The Rebels' center kicked the puck toward the boards. From behind him, the Rebels' right defenseman raced to the puck.

So did I.

I got there first. I chipped the puck ahead along the boards, past the defenseman, and I chased the puck into the corner.

I knew where Nate would go. That's why they called me Radar. Because I saw the entire ice and knew how all the plays would unfold.

Yes, Nate was in a traffic jam in front of the net, but he knew what I knew: where the open ice was. Back at the top of the face-off circle, where I had just been. It would be open there. He'd have time to shoot.

I glanced up the boards and saw the defenseman racing for me. The safe pass was to bounce it off the boards knee high, back to our defenseman at the point. But time was ticking. A goal this late in the game would almost guarantee us a win.

I floated a pass to the top of the face-off circle.

Except Nate wasn't there!

Instead the Rebels' center stepped in and took my pass. He had some momentum and used it to peel away up the ice, toward our defenseman on the point.

The Rebels' center saw that our defenseman had come in a little too far, expecting my pass. With his speed, the center knew our defenseman was trapped. The center banged the puck off the boards past the defenseman and burst over the blue line.

The center poured on the speed, breaking

loose. All alone on the goalie.

He moved right and then left; then he flicked the puck up and over our goalie's shoulder into our net.

Just like that, we were down 4–3. Worse, we'd given up a shorthanded goal.

Correction. I'd given up a shorthanded goal because of a bad pass.

I hung my head and skated back toward the players' box. I didn't want to be able to read any lips as I took myself off the ice.

 # Eight

About twenty-four hours after causing the Hitmen to lose the opening game of the season, I was standing on a street corner near a theater in the Kensington shopping district of Calgary. The weather had stayed nice, and on this evening a lot of people were walking the streets.

Kensington is an older area of Calgary, across the Bow River from the downtown skyscrapers, with a lot of cool shops and restaurants. It was the kind of area Nate liked. Fancy people in fancy clothes driving fancy cars. Not my kind of place.

I was wearing jeans and a beat-up leather jacket. Nate, who had already gone into the theater, had on some designer jeans and an expensive leather jacket. I knew this because I'd been following him down the street from a safe distance so he couldn't see me. In the last few months, he'd spent a lot of money on clothes. Which made me wonder, of course, where the money had come from.

It surprised me that he was going to see a movie. I'd expected something else when I'd driven to the house where he was billeted during the season.

Nate had driven straight to Kensington in his late-model Ford pickup. I'd kept some cars between us, and it wasn't a problem following him in my old Camry.

My problem was wondering why two guys in a bright red Mustang had delivered a thousand dollars in cash for him. It seemed obvious that Nate was doing something illegal. Especially because he wasn't talking about it to me.

We'll see you tomorrow night. Usual time. Usual place.

That's what the guys had said just before handing me the envelope. *We'll see you tomorrow night. Usual time. Usual place.*

Since I didn't know the time or place, the only way to find out was by watching Nate until he met them. Maybe then I'd learn what all this was about.

A touch on my elbow broke through my thoughts.

I turned to see who was holding my arm. I was surprised to see a girl—tall, like me. About my age too. With long, burnished copper hair. Freckles. And a very, very nice smile. Wearing jeans and a sweater and a leather jacket that wasn't as beat up as mine.

Yup. Mercedes.

Surprised as I was to see her, I was even more surprised when she leaned close and gave me a kiss on the cheek.

"Great to see you," she said. Her voice was velvet, even filtered through my cochlear implant.

Wow, I thought, I must have really impressed her at the tournament when I gave away all the gambling money. I'd make sure to tell Nate that. Then he'd finally understand I had done the right thing.

"Great to see you too," I said. I felt shy.

In the street's light, it was easy to see the frown on her face.

What had I said wrong?

"Nolan?" she said slowly.

I nodded. This suddenly seemed to be going in the wrong direction.

"I am so sorry," she said. "I thought you were Nate."

Oh. It wasn't *what* I'd said that was wrong. It was *how* I'd said it. As in the way a guy with a hearing difficulty speaks. Instead of the way that a guy in designer jeans and an expensive leather jacket speaks.

"Don't worry about it," I said. I wanted to crawl into a sewer grate. It would have been easy. I felt only a couple of inches tall. "It happens a lot."

She shook her head. "No, I should have noticed quicker. Nate's not as big in the chest as you are."

She looked down. Then up. She had a big purse, which she held as if to protect herself from me. "I didn't mean it to sound that way. Like I've studied you or anything."

"Don't worry about it," I said. I'm sure what she meant is that she'd spent a lot of time studying Nate. He must have called her after the golf tournament. Not that I would have known, since he and I weren't speaking to each other.

"It's just that I was expecting to meet Nate at the theater," she said. "I didn't know you would be here. So I assumed it was Nate I saw on the street and that you hadn't made it to the movie yet."

"Nate's here?" I said, doing my best to sound surprised. I didn't want Nate to know I'd been following him. "Small town, I guess."

"Yeah," she said. "Small town."

"Well," I said, "let's make a deal. Don't tell Nate I was here. Then you won't have to explain that you kissed the wrong guy."

She held out her hand to shake mine.

"Deal," she said. She gave a quick embarrassed smile. "See you later."

She walked away to the theater.

I waited a few minutes and then I hurried after her. Now it looked like I'd be following Nate and Mercedes for the night.

 # Nine

At least Nate had picked a decent movie for his date with Mercedes. It was the opening night of an action-packed thriller with car chases and buildings getting blown up. It had been advertised for months ahead of time, and there was a showing of it every two hours. The theater was packed, and lots of people were waiting in line.

That was the other piece of good news. Because there were so many people, it was easy for me to slip into the back row and feel certain that Nate and Mercedes wouldn't see me there. After all, if I was going to follow Nate until I found out what *the usual time and place* meant, I'd rather be somewhere where I could enjoy my wait.

Except it turned out I was wrong about the enjoyment part.

Ever noticed that the more exciting the trailer for a movie is, the more boring it turns out to be? This was one of those movies.

Still, I had popcorn and something to drink. Nate and Mercedes were sitting a few rows ahead of me, and I was able to keep a close watch on them.

During one of the few good parts of the movie—a car chase with explosions and jumps over destroyed bridges and through machine gun fire—Nate left his seat.

He stepped into the aisle and started walking toward the exit behind me.

How could he leave at the best part?

It made me suspicious. If you have to take a bathroom break at a movie, you wait until the slow music plays and the main female character starts telling the main male character that she's falling in love with him.

I ducked my head as Nate passed. It was unlikely that he'd notice me in the dark packed theater, but I wasn't going to take the chance.

I counted to ten; then I slipped out of my row too.

I walked to the exit at the back and slowly stepped into the lobby.

No sign of Nate.

Now what?

There were people in line for popcorn and drinks, so I decided to take the chance that I wouldn't be too obvious if I quickly walked across to the video game machines set up in the far corner. I sat in front of a race-car game and grabbed the fake steering wheel.

Then I looked around again.

Had Nate really decided he needed to go to the washroom?

I kept my eyes on the door to the men's washroom. It struck me that maybe the meeting was in there. Right after that it struck me that I'd watched too many spy movies.

As I watched the door, however, someone did walk quickly to the washroom from the far side of the lobby. A tall man with thinning hair, wearing a theater employees' uniform.

Yeah, I told myself. Too many spy movies.

Especially when Nate walked out about thirty seconds later. He went straight back into the theater.

So I'd missed the best part of the movie for nothing.

I got up from the race-car game and headed back to the theater. As I did, the tall man with thinning hair came out of the washroom.

I'm no expert on how long it should or shouldn't take for guys to go to the bathroom. Still, it seemed that the guy had done his business really quickly.

Unless his business had been with Nate.

I told myself again that I'd watched too many spy movies. Still, if I'd made an idiot of myself so far, there was no harm in being an idiot a little longer.

I slowed down and stayed behind the line of people getting popcorn. I didn't want this guy to see my face, just in case he really had gone in there to meet Nate.

I joined the last person in line and kept watching the tall guy. He didn't look from side to side, just hurried back through the lobby the same way he'd hurried to the washroom.

At the far side of the lobby, he disappeared through a door.

Again, I counted to ten. Then I checked it out.

There was a small sign on the door: *EM-PLOYEES ONLY. PROJECTOR ROOM.*

That explained why the guy had been in such a hurry. If you're in charge of making sure the movie is running, you don't want to be away from it for long.

At least I'd learned one thing: The time and place for Nate's meeting wasn't here. Now I'd have to follow him after the movie.

As I slipped back into the theater to find my place, I realized something else. If Mercedes stayed with him and met the two guys in the expensive Mustang convertible, that would probably mean she was part of it too.

Whatever *it* was.

 Ten

After the movie finished, Nate walked out with Mercedes. I joined the crowd leaving the theater and stayed far enough behind so they wouldn't notice me.

Outside it was cooler than at the beginning of the evening. It was still pleasant though, and the sidewalks were crowded with people. That made it easier to stay with Nate and Mercedes without being noticed.

I was afraid they'd go to a restaurant. That would mean standing around outside for an hour or more with nothing to do.

I was relieved when they walked to Nate's truck, about half a block down from my car. I was pleased when he tried to hold her hand, and she pulled away. I told myself I wasn't jealous.

When they drove off, I jumped into my Toyota.

From Kensington, he drove along the north side of the river. After a few minutes, he turned right onto the low level bridge to cross the river to downtown. Above it was another bridge guarded by a big statue of a lion on each side. It seemed like the lions were scowling at me.

Maybe I deserved it.

I told myself that I was following my brother to find out what kind of trouble he was in so that I could rescue him. Not because I wanted to prove he was in trouble, but because I had been jealous of him my whole life. He was fast. Slick. In the limelight. It never seemed fair that we were as close to identical from head to toe as two humans can be, but I was the one who had started losing my hearing for no reason that any doctor could find, and he was the one with normal hearing, a normal speaking voice and no implant.

In my car, I looked up and scowled back at the lions.

Across the river, Nate turned into Calgary's Chinatown. In the first week after I got to Calgary, Nate had taken me to a great restaurant in Chinatown. I had loved the food. There was an energy in Chinatown that I loved too—the bright neon signs, people on the sidewalks, busy traffic, horns honking.

Nate slowed down and signaled that he was going to back into a parking spot.

Nuts.

The street was jammed with traffic, and I couldn't see any open parking spots between my car and his truck. A car behind me honked, because it looked like I was slowing down for no reason.

I had no choice but to move along and hope that Nate didn't notice my car as I passed his truck. I hunched down and kept going. There was another parking spot half a block away.

Should I take it?

I checked my rearview mirror and saw that Nate had jumped from his truck and gone into a small video store between two restaurants.

So I pulled into the open spot.

Now what?

Was he renting a movie?

But why in Chinatown? That wasn't close to where his billets lived. And the movie rental place had Chinese characters on the windows, like it specialized in Chinese language movies.

Why rent there?

I decided to wait in my car and keep watching in my rearview mirror. If he was just renting a movie, I needed to be in a good position if

I was going to keep following him. If he wasn't renting a movie, maybe I'd see the two guys from the Mustang go in or out of the shop.

I sat in my Camry, just a few parking spots ahead of Nate's truck. The streetlights showed clearly that Mercedes was still sitting in his truck. It was more fun to watch her than the sidewalk.

I frowned.

She had pulled a video camera from her lap. Had it been in her purse?

She swung the camera toward the video store and pointed it at the store window for a few seconds. Her lips were moving.

She was talking as she recorded?

I stared as hard as I could. It wasn't daylight, and even with the streetlights I couldn't be sure that I was seeing every lip movement. Still, I was pretty sure I could make sense of it.

"Nate Andrews has run into this movie rental place," she said. "He didn't want to discuss why. It will be interesting to see if he comes out with a movie. The two men speaking to him are not Asian. I doubt they work in the video store."

Then she pulled the camera down. It disappeared below the dash of the truck as if she were putting it back into her purse.

Now this was getting truly weird.

Before I could give it any thought, a big biker guy showed up at my driver's side window. The big blond guy with tattoos who had given me money to give to Nate.

He bent down and looked at me. Then he tapped on the window. With a tire iron.

"Step outside," he said. "If you don't, I'll break the window."

I've read that the best time to resist during a mugging is in the first few seconds. I was going to slide across to the passenger side and try to make a run for it down the sidewalk. The guy with the tire iron was huge. But probably not fast. If I couldn't outrun him, I didn't belong in the WHL.

But someone else was waiting on the other side of my car. The other guy from the Mustang. Just as big. Just as mean-looking. With a bent nose.

I didn't have much choice.

I got out of the car.

Eleven

"Kid," Tattoo Biker said to me, "this is the end of the line for you."

If he meant it as a joke, he wasn't smiling.

Neither was I. We were standing near the LRT tracks by the river, not far from downtown. LRT stands for Light Rail Transit. Calgary's C-train. It's part of the transit system, but it uses trains instead of buses. The trains came and went about every ten minutes.

I hoped he didn't mean what I thought he meant about the end of the line. I was having a hard time keeping my balance, and there was no way I could make a run for it.

After taking me from my car, they had put me in a white van. Once I was inside, they had used duct tape to wrap my wrists and my ankles. Then Tattoo Biker had started driving, with me in the back.

No matter how many questions I'd asked, they'd said nothing. They'd gone through some alleys and ended up near the river. The tracks were fenced off, but they'd used wire cutters to get through. Then they had carried me like a sack of rocks to a place near the track. Finally they had put me on my feet again.

Tattoo Biker was holding what looked like a long unlit flashlight with two points sticking out of the front of it. The tracks were well lit. I wondered why he needed the flashlight. He saw me looking at it and gave his first smile.

"It's a flashlight stun gun," he said. "Know how it works?"

"Better be simple," I said, "or an idiot like you doesn't have a chance."

Not the smartest thing to say, but I hate bullies.

Tattoo Biker proved it wasn't the smartest thing to say.

He shoved the stun gun into me.

Once, when I was too little to know better, I had pushed the end of a screwdriver into an electrical outlet. That's what it felt like. Except a hundred times worse.

I screamed and barely managed to keep my balance.

"That's only a half-second jolt," Tattoo Biker said. "It gets worse."

Bent Nose Biker stepped forward and wrapped something around my head. A blindfold.

"Doing this for your own good," Bent Nose Biker said with a laugh. "That way you won't see it coming."

I didn't have to ask what I wouldn't see. I felt them lift me and put me on the tracks.

He meant the train.

"Any chance you guys will change your mind about this?" I asked.

"None," Tattoo Biker said.

"Probably a good thing," I said. "You'd need a diaper to do it."

"Huh?" he said.

"If you're going to change your mind, you'll need a diaper," I said. "Let me explain. It's a joke. It means that your brain is full of "

He jabbed me longer and harder with the stun gun. Now it was a thousand times worse. I fell to my knees on the track. I had no control over my muscles. My magnetic spider had been knocked off my head. My world went silent.

They shifted my body so that I was all the way across the tracks. I still couldn't move.

In my world of silence, I wondered if getting hit by the train would hurt. Maybe what

51

the preacher had told me in grade five about the cement truck hitting my parents' car had been true. Maybe I really wouldn't feel a thing. I began to pray that the preacher was right. About not feeling the pain. And about going to a better place. I concentrated on praying. I was afraid of discovering how terrified I was.

I didn't have long to pray. Rumbling told me that a train was approaching.

The rumble didn't come as noise. It came as a vibration that hummed in my chest. Even though I was blindfolded, I turned my head toward the train, as if I needed my eyes to tell me what I already knew.

The train was close and coming fast. With me on the tracks.

Louder and louder. Faster and faster.

I braced for impact. What else could I do?

I wasn't that brave. I screamed.

Suddenly something yanked me off the tracks. The train whizzed by as hands lifted me to my feet.

The blindfold was pulled off. I was shaking so hard I had to bite down to keep my teeth from shattering.

I saw the end of the train disappear down the tracks. I felt the spider hanging loosely from my processor. I tilted my head, and the magnetic spider landed on my skull and clicked back into place.

"Thought you were dead, didn't you?" Tattoo Biker said.

Sound was back in my life. *Life*. What a sweet word.

I didn't answer. I was afraid I'd say something smart-mouthed again. Much as I hate bullies, sometimes a person really should keep his mouth shut. Especially after discovering how good it was to be alive. But I also knew I wasn't talking because I couldn't find my voice. All I could think of was those final seconds when I had thought a train was going to slam into me.

Tattoo Biker and Bent Nose Biker lifted me again and carried me through the fence.

Bent Nose Biker pulled out a switchblade. Snapped it open. He pointed the blade at me. Then he cut through the tape around my wrists.

"We're going," Tattoo Biker said. "You can take the tape off your ankles. Just remember to stay away from the video place. Next time, we won't pull you off the tracks. Got it?"

I stared at them and said nothing as they walked away. It would not be good to make them mad again.

 # Twelve

Coach Jon had called me into his office. Alone. Never a good sign. I gave him my frequency monitor to wear around his neck. My FM. It hung from a thin cord and was smaller than a cigarette lighter. The FM is part of the system that lets me hear. It has a built-in microphone that sends sound to my processor.

"Radar," Coach Jon said, "remind me again why the Hitmen worked so hard to get you traded to this team."

I wanted to make a smart remark. Something about how the Hitmen were equal opportunity employers and they needed someone with a disability to get government grant money. I know that sounds cold, but what were people thinking when they set up special programs like that? From my point of view, deaf people don't need special treatment. We don't. Nor do we need people feeling sorry for us.

Say you did get work because of that kind of program. Everyone around you would assume you were there only because you were different. That doesn't get you much respect. No, the only way to get respect is to earn it. Don't hire me because I'm different. Hire me because I can work hard, and I'm smart enough to do a job like everybody else. Period. It's why I like hockey. No special treatment.

Not that all of that went through my head when Coach Jon asked why the Hitmen had traded for me. All I really thought about was how maybe the Hitmen wanted government grant money. But unless someone was trying to push me around, I usually kept my mouth shut. I quickly pushed the thought away and answered his question politely.

"I know you wanted me to play with my brother."

"Tell me why we wanted you to play with your brother."

I don't always need the FM. I use it in noisy areas or in important meetings. It has a range of about two hundred feet. What's really important to my hearing is the processor that hangs from my ear. It looks like a Bluetooth headset for a cell phone. I can use the FM to send sound signals to it. If the FM is shut off, sound reaches me through the three built-in microphones in the processor. There is also a mini-computer inside that sends audio signals to my spider.

Here's where it gets really cool. The spider stays in place outside my skull because a magnet inside the spider attaches to another magnet that was implanted in my skull during the operation. From the implant under my skull, long microfibers containing twenty-two electrodes are threaded into my cochlea, the part of the inner ear that translates sound vibrations. If the spider is not attached to my head, I can't hear a thing. At home, when I take it off to sleep, I just attach it to the fridge, like any other magnetic sticker.

I answered Coach Jon's question. "You wanted me to play on a team with my brother because together we have a good scoring record."

"And why do you have a good scoring record?" he asked, very patiently. "Do I need to give you a hint? *Radar*?"

By the way he said my nickname, I knew he was using it as the hint. But I'd known all along what he wanted to hear.

"Nate and I make good passing plays," I said.

"Correction," Coach Jon said. "You and Nate *used* to make good passing plays. I've seen video footage of you playing together before you both began in the WHL. It gave me goose bumps. Not only are you guys good as individual players, but you are spooky good when you work together. It's like you're one hockey player in two bodies."

I'd heard that before. A lot. It used to make me feel good.

"His scoring touch was amazing when you fed him passes," Coach Jon said. "And every one of your passes used to hit the tape of his stick like you had radar."

I heard what he was saying. *Had* radar. Not *have* radar. As in it used to be there but wasn't anymore.

Coach Jon was shaking his head. Not mad. But still with amazement. "For the first week of practices, you guys were unbelievable," he said. "Even that stunt you pulled at the Hitmen golf tournament showed great teamwork."

"Stunt?"

He rolled his eyes. "You think just because I wasn't there I don't know what happened? I loved hearing about it. I would have paid good money to see Bob Jones get fooled like that."

Coach Jon's smiled faded. "But now you guys are just a couple of clowns on the ice. For years—a perfect team. Then overnight—clowns. That's why I called you into my office. I want to help you guys fix this. Whatever the problem is. But I can't help until you tell me what happened."

What happened was that my brother was keeping something from me, and I couldn't trust him anymore.

I shrugged. "It's just a slump, I guess."

"Don't lie to me," Coach Jon said mildly. "I called all your previous coaches. Back to when you both started playing hockey. None of them remembers anything like this happening to you guys before."

Coach Jon leaned forward, his heavy forearms on his desk. "What's gone wrong between the two of you? Is it a girl?"

"No," I said, "just a slump."

He stared at me. Good thing he couldn't read my mind.

Finally he sighed.

"If that's the way you want it to be," he said. "It doesn't make me feel better, but at least you and Nate are working as a team in this area."

"Sir?"

"I had him in the office half an hour ago. He

says it must be a slump too."

"Oh."

"Look," Coach Jon said. "It's obvious that you and Nate won't let me help with whatever is wrong here. If I can't do anything about it, then it's not *our* problem. It's *your* problem."

Coach Jon stood and leaned across his desk, his weight on his palms.

"You guys are choosing to make it your problem," Coach Jon said. "Fix it. Soon. Or both of you are going to see about as much ice time as the team mascot."

 # Thirteen

W hen I looked into the rearview mirror of my car, I didn't recognize myself. It was amazing what thirty dollars spent in a costume store could do.

I was parked at a meter in Chinatown, just down from the video store between the two restaurants. I needed that one last look in the mirror to make sure my disguise would work. After all, if the guys in the rental place were in on whatever Nate was doing, I wouldn't get too far if I looked nearly identical to him when I walked in to rent a movie. So I'd found a costume shop a few blocks away and spent that thirty dollars.

I now had a blond mustache, glued in place. I was wearing a ball cap with long straggly blond hair sticking out—the hair was glued to the inside of the ball cap. The hair hid my processor and spider. I wore cheap sunglasses. I even had some fake teeth in place that hurt where they rubbed against my gums.

Good thing there wasn't anyone around to tell me that my own mother would not have recognized me. Even all these years after sitting down in the principal's office to hear the bad news from the minister, it hurt whenever someone or something reminded me of her.

I pushed open the car door and walked down the sidewalk. The temperature was dropping as the sun set. A wind was coming from the west as it usually did, dropping masses of air down the side of the mountains before pushing across the prairies.

I stopped on the street just before going inside the video store. There were no English words on the windows or the door. The movie posters taped inside the window had Chinese characters. It looked weird, seeing a *Star Wars* poster with writing that I couldn't begin to understand unless I studied it for years.

I doubted Nate understood the Chinese characters either. Or any words in Chinese. Which made me wonder all over again what he had been doing inside the shop.

I stepped inside. A bell rang. A guy came out

of the back room and up to the counter. He was a couple of years older than me. He was skinny with a buzz cut, and he wore a tight black T-shirt. His ropy arms had tattoos on the biceps.

He looked at me for only a second. Then he sat on a stool behind the counter and pulled out a magazine. I caught a flash of the cover—some kind of motorcycle. I couldn't read the headlines, but even from the other side of the store I saw it was in English.

I began looking at titles. They were probably in alphabetical order, but since they were in Chinese, it was only a guess.

I glanced back at the counter. The guy dropped his head, as if I'd caught him looking at me.

There was no chance I could convince him that I was here for one of the movies in front of me. But I had planned for that. There was one kind of movie where it really didn't matter if you couldn't understand Chinese. Some of them even had English subtitles.

"Hey," I said to Counter Guy as I moved toward him. "Got any Bruce Lee movies?"

"You like Bruce Lee?" Counter Guy said. "Cool." Bruce Lee was a martial arts fighter a long time ago. One of the best. A legend. He made movies in China that became popular here. He died mysteriously in Hong Kong when he was really young.

Counter Guy pointed to another part of the store. That's when I got a closer look at the tattoos on his biceps. One of the tattoos was a grinning pirate's face with crossbones. Exactly like the tattoos on the two bikers who had taken me onto the tracks of the C-train.

I hoped I kept my face from showing any shock. I walked to where he had pointed.

I passed a small display of movies in English. It looked like a top twenty list of movies that had just been released on DVD. I stopped and stared for a second or two. The prices on the cases looked low compared to what I'd seen in other stores.

I felt a bit of hope. Maybe that's why Nate had come in. He liked the restaurants around here. He liked movies. He knew about this place and that it carried recent releases. My hope faded as I wondered why Mercedes had been videotaping him. And why did the guy behind the counter have the same tattoos as the bikers?

I wandered over to the Bruce Lee movies and pretended I was interested. I had just learned something. I didn't know what it meant yet. I'd stay a few minutes longer so it would look like I really had stopped by to check out Bruce Lee movies.

The bell sounded as the door opened again. I looked up. And suddenly wished I could jump over the counter and hide in the back room.

I knew the person walking into the store. Mercedes.

 # Fourteen

S he was wearing jeans and a Calgary Flames hockey jersey. She carried a huge purse, just like on her date with Nate. I wondered if it still held a video camera.

She ignored me and breezed past me to the counter.

"I'd like to buy a DVD," she said. She named the movie that she had just seen with Nate.

"Sorry," Counter Guy said. "That just hit the theaters. It's not available yet on DVD."

"I was talking to a friend," she said. "She said I could get it here."

"Your friend is wrong."

"She goes out with someone who plays for the Hitmen," she said. "Do I need to give you his name?"

There were a few seconds of silence. I had my back to them, pretending to study the Bruce Lee movies.

"Maybe come back in a few minutes," Counter Guy finally said. "I'll phone my boss and see what he knows."

"A few minutes?" she asked.

"Just a few minutes."

I understood what he meant. In a few minutes, when the store didn't have anyone else in it.

I picked up and dropped a couple of the Bruce Lee movies. The plastic cases clattered in the silence.

"Sorry!" I said without looking back at them.

I squatted to pick them up. With my hands in front of me, I slid my FM behind one of the DVD cases before I put them all back.

I turned back to the two of them. I shrugged and walked out. I hoped that Mercedes hadn't recognized my voice.

Outside the store, I walked down the sidewalk about twenty steps. I made sure I was still in range of my FM.

In elementary school, sometimes teachers who wore it for me would forget to turn it off when they left the classroom. In the staffroom or the washroom, I'd be able to hear them, because the FM transmitted sounds to my processor, even if I was in another room. I can tell you that it changes how you think about a sweet old lady teacher after you have heard her on the toilet talking to herself about hoping the prune juice would deliver more than a good toot. It changes even more after you've heard something from her on the toilet right after that. Something loud and rude, like a startled duck quacking when you step on it. Something you want to make sure you don't smell. Yup. A good toot. That was in grade four. Every time I looked at her for the rest of the year, I giggled, and she didn't know why.

That's how I knew my FM transmitter in the video store would pick up the conversation between Mercedes and Counter Guy. It would be as clear to me as if I were still standing there.

"Okay," she said. "We're alone."

"Did you see that guy's goofy hair?" Counter Guy said. "And that lame mustache?"

"The movie," she replied. "You've got it, right? My girlfriend goes out with Nate, who plays for the Hitmen. I'm sure this is the place she was talking about."

"The DVD is going to cost you twenty-five dollars."

"That's steep," she said.

"Hey," he said. "It won't be out on a commercial DVD for a few months. You can always wait."

"I don't know," she answered. "It still seems

like a lot."

"Get a few of your friends to chip in," he said. "Watch it together. It will still be cheaper than going to a theater."

"Well," she said. "Now that you put it that way."

"Cash only," he said.

Cash. Like the cash that Nate had these days?

"Right," Mercedes said. "It's in here somewhere."

I heard rustling. She must have found the cash in her huge bag, because the next thing I heard was the sound of a movie case being plunked down on the counter.

"Thanks," he said. "Don't suppose you're looking for a boyfriend?"

"Wouldn't be you if I was," Mercedes said.

"Hey," he said. "I make plenty of money. We could go to a lot of cool places."

"Yeah," she said. "Remember your comment about that guy's goofy hair and lame mustache?"

"You liked *him*?"

"I don't even know him," she said. "But I don't like people who judge other people by appearances. You might have money, but it doesn't make up for being mean."

"Fine," he said. "You don't sound like much

68

fun anyway."

She didn't answer. A second later, I heard the bell over the door ring. Then I saw her step onto the sidewalk outside the store. She turned away from me, so I didn't have to worry about hiding from her.

I did have to worry about something else.

My FM was still in the movie rental place. It was worth a lot of money. I couldn't leave it behind. I'd have to go back in and tell the guy I'd gone to my car to get my wallet. Then I'd have to pick out one of the Bruce Lee DVDs and pay for it. I sure didn't want him guessing what I had done or what I had learned.

Halfway back to the door, I froze at a new sound that reached me from inside the store. The sound was loud and rude, like a startled duck quacking when you step on it. Something you want to make sure you don't smell.

"Dude," Counter Guy said to himself. "Good one!"

Then a few seconds later, he coughed and gagged and muttered, "Dude, bad one. Trying to commit suicide?"

I decided to wait a few more minutes before I went back into the store. It was a small store. I wanted to make sure the air had cleared out before I went in for a movie. I wasn't interested in any bonus features.

Fifteen

I went into a corner against the defenseman for the Lethbridge Hurricanes. No matter how badly he wanted to win the fight for the puck, I knew I wanted it worse.

Five minutes into overtime, we hadn't lost our second game of the season. Yet. The score was 3–3. Next goal won the game.

We were playing the Hurricanes in their building. Lethbridge is only a few hours away from Calgary; it was an away game against them. We would play them on our home ice the next night.

I couldn't speak for the rest of the team, but I felt some desperation. We should have easily won the game already. Things seemed out of sync though. For all lines. But especially ours.

With me at left wing and Nate at center, that left "Rooster" Joe MacAllister on right wing. We called him Rooster because he had bright red hair that no amount of hair gel could tame.

Rooster was a fighter. Quick-tempered in a way that surprised no one when they saw his hair color.

All night, we'd been missing opportunities. Passes going into skates instead of stick blades. Weak shots on net. Falling into the corners. Of the three Hitmen goals, our line had contributed zero points. Of the three Lethbridge goals against us, our line had been on the ice for two.

Bad as we had been all night, I told myself, it was going to end now.

I went into the corner hard. The defenseman had turned his body to protect the puck. He brought up an elbow that stung my jaw.

No quitting!

I wasn't worried about damage to my cochlear implant. I never worried about it. Not that things couldn't go wrong. Some parents might never have let a kid with an implant go to the level of hockey that I played. Hockey was a sport where your head could get banged around, and there was always the chance it would damage not only the implant, but me.

My parents were dead, and in my foster

homes there were plenty of other things for adults to worry about, so continuing in hockey was not something I had to fight for. The cochlear implant? In one way, of course, I cared. I didn't want it damaged, and I didn't want to lose the hearing that it gave me. My helmet had extra padding, and I didn't wear the spider or processor during games, so that lessened the risk.

But if I let fear dictate how to live my life, I would be giving in to a different kind of bully. I hate bullies. I wasn't going to let my hearing loss stop me from facing challenges. Early on I had decided to take the risk.

So when that elbow stung my jaw hard, I dug in to fight even harder for the puck. I hoped the referee would call a penalty. Not that I'd be able to hear him blow the whistle, since I wasn't wearing either my spider or my processor.

If the Hurricanes' defenseman relaxed, then the whistle had ended the play.

He didn't relax. No penalty.

He fought just as hard for the puck as I did.

Didn't matter. I wanted it more.

Two seconds later, I chipped it out from his skates and sent it farther down the boards.

Quick glance for Nate. All through our playing career, I had only needed a quick glance.

Sometimes, not even that. My radar for his presence was something I wasn't ever able to explain, not even to myself. The closest I could get was that we were twins. Maybe our bond had become even stronger after we were orphaned and knew we could depend only on each other.

Still, the radar was spooky. Always had been. That's what had made us almost legendary at every level we had played together. That's why the Hitmen had gone to so much trouble to put us together.

Except tonight, like at the last game, it wasn't working. I couldn't tell where Nate was. Not without looking around too long and giving up the puck that I'd just fought so hard to get.

I put my head down and scooped the puck.

I didn't want to give up a bad pass, so I held on to it. Normally that wasn't my style. I was a passer, a set-up man. Nate did the fancy stuff.

Where was he?

I spun in a tight circle. The Hurricanes' right winger moved in on me, covering for the defenseman.

I faked my shoulders one way, moved my hips the other. Just like that, I was clear. For a second.

Then I spotted Nate. He'd drifted to the other side of the net.

I raced for the top of the face-off circle with the puck. Nate was waiting. Like always. There was a gap to feed him the puck. If I snapped the pass, he'd be in a great position to flick it into the net before the goalie turned. We'd win with an overtime goal.

Instead I felt a surge of anger. Why give him the glory game after game? How many times did he pass me the puck? Hadn't I just proven I could hold onto the puck and get through traffic?

I held on longer. The Hurricanes' center was dogging me. I spun again. All I needed to do was get clear of him and then fake a pass to Nate and instead, wrist the puck to the other side of the net.

Yeah. The deaf guy could be a hero for a change.

Except as I spun, I lost the puck.

The Hurricanes' center was like a wolf on a helpless rabbit, snagging the puck and churning up ice in a burst of speed that left me standing as if someone had tied my skates together.

His wingers joined him.

Nate was still back at the Hurricanes' net, waiting for a pass. Which left him badly out of position.

It gave the Hurricanes a three-on-two rush

against our defenseman. That began a three-on-one when our right defenseman caught the edge of his skate in a crack on the ice and fell.

Five seconds later, the Hurricanes scored.

I felt my shoulders slump. Then I felt someone slap my shoulder from behind.

I turned.

It was Nate.

He was yelling. I couldn't hear him, of course. But I was able to read his lips.

"What were you thinking? I was wide open! Why didn't you pass?"

"I'm learning from you," I said. At that moment, I didn't like him very much. Thinking about his involvement with a bunch of bikers.

He skated in closer, yelling more words that were easy to read on his lips. "What? Learning what?"

"Learning how to be a puck hog," I said. I was mad about losing the puck. Mad about losing the game. Mad about losing my temper. "So maybe you should start to learn from me."

He stared at me, his eyes bugging.

"Yeah," I said. "Any time you have the puck, I make sure I'm in position to head back up the ice to make a defensive play, because you might lose the puck. Maybe you should start doing the same when I have the puck. Or maybe start passing to me when I'm open. Until then, good luck getting anything from me."

I wouldn't have guessed it would be possible for his eyes to bug out any farther, but they did.

He grabbed my shoulder.

I shook off his hand. If he was going to fight, I was ready.

That's when Rooster stepped between us. Nate skated away. I followed.

Even though the trip between Lethbridge and Calgary is one of the shortest in the league, the bus ride back home seemed to take forever.

 # Sixteen

I found Nate in the high school cafeteria the next morning. He was pouring ketchup on a plate of scrambled eggs. Three girls were sitting at his table, all giggling at a joke he had just told. At least I hoped it was a joke.

That's how bad it was between us.

A year ago, I would have trusted him enough to let him dangle me from the top of the Calgary Tower. Now I wondered if he had seen me walking toward the table and had said something to them about his stupid, deaf twin brother that made them laugh.

I stood beside the table. I didn't say anything.

"Where's your breakfast?" Nate asked.

"Not hungry," I said. I didn't move. I didn't smile.

The girls took the hint. They left with their trays.

"You sure know how to bring the mood

down," Nate said. "I was having fun."

"Really?" I said. I had a folded *Calgary Sun* in my back pocket. "I'm not."

I tossed the *Calgary Sun* onto the table and sat down beside him. "Check out the sports section."

He did. He knew instantly what I wanted him to read. The headline popped out from the page: *TWINS TO BE SEPARATED*?

I gave him time to read the entire article. It was about how Nate and I had not even come close to meeting all the pre-season expectations after I was traded to the Hitmen. It pointed out that not only were we failing to help the team, we were failing the team. It suggested that it was time for one of us to be traded away from the Hitmen before we became complete embarrassments as linemates. At the very least, it said, we should be playing on different lines.

The cafeteria was half full. Maybe I was giving off a bad vibe. Or an intense vibe. No one stopped by the table to chat.

"It's like they think we're Siamese twins," Nate said. "Like it's major surgery to trade one of us to another team."

I stared at him coldly. "Obviously you don't think it's a big deal."

"I've got my life," he said. "You've got yours."

"I always thought," I said, "that after Mom and Dad got killed, all we had was each other."

He stared back just as coldly. "That was what we told each other in the dark when we were just kids. You know, back when it was okay to cry. I don't cry anymore. So don't you think it's time to grow up and do your own thing?"

"I think that if one of us needs help, the other one should be there. Always. No matter what."

"Fine," he said. "If you need help, ask."

"I don't need help," I said.

"Well, I don't either," he said. "So I guess there's nothing to discuss."

He stood.

I grabbed his arm and pulled him back down. He pulled his fist back like he was going to hit me.

I looked at his hand. He looked at his hand. He let out a breath.

"I wasn't going to hit you," he said. "Really."

This time, I stood.

"You don't need to hit me," I said. "You've already done enough damage."

I left him at the table, with a plateful of cold scrambled eggs, staring at the *Calgary Sun*.

TWINS TO BE SEPARATED?

I knew the answer. We already were.

Seventeen

Mercedes was leaning against my Camry when I got out of school that afternoon.

The postcard-perfect weather had continued. Not even a tiny breeze moved her hair. She looked postcard perfect too in a white hoodie, jeans and cowboy boots. She had set her big purse on the hood of my car.

"Sorry," I said quickly when I reached her. "Wrong guy again. I'm Nolan."

On the one hand, there was something about her that made my heart speed up when I saw her. On the other hand, I had five fingers. I know—bad joke. Really, on the other hand, she had gone out with Nate. And because of all the strange things that were happening, I didn't trust her. So I guess my voice was a little cold when I said that to her.

Her small smile became a straight line as she pressed her lips together briefly. Then she put the smile back on her face.

"I deserve that," she said. "But I'm here because I wanted to talk to you. Not Nate."

"Sure," I said. Something was bothering me about this. How had she known this Camry was mine? "Let's talk."

"Don't be like that," she said.

"Like what?"

"Like you really don't want to talk."

"It's been a long day," I said. It had been. I kept seeing that headline in my mind. *TWINS TO BE SEPARATED*? Except, of course, in my mind the headline didn't end with a question mark.

"I've had a long day too," she said. "I didn't know if I should come to you with this or not. But in the end, you were the only person I thought I could trust. And even if it hurts you, I thought you were the kind of guy who would rather know than not know."

"I'm listening," I said. Only because doctors had once put an implant into my skull.

She looked around the parking lot. "Maybe we should go for a drive."

"Um, I'm pretty busy." This wasn't true. But if we went for a drive, we'd be alone together. I didn't want the part of me that thought she was cute to overwhelm the part of me that didn't trust her. "Can you just tell me about it here?"

"We shouldn't be seen together," she said. "Trust me."

That was my problem. I couldn't. I didn't say that though.

"Which one is your car?" I asked. She must have driven here.

She pointed at a black Volkswagen Beetle. It was at least a few years old. It had a cracked windshield and some dings in the front left fender.

"Let's go," I said, moving toward it.

"What's wrong with your car?" she asked.

I was surprised. What girl would want to drive around in an old wreck like mine? "Are you serious? Look at it."

"It's clean," she said. "It runs. Isn't that all that matters?"

"To me," I said. "But other people…"

"I'm not other people."

So I unlocked the passenger side door for her. I walked around to unlock my door, but she had already leaned across and unlocked it from the inside.

When I started the car, my music began playing. I turned it down.

"Dire Straits," she said. "I love that band."

She knew about Dire Straits? A British group from the seventies and eighties. Decades ago.

"It's rock but without a hundred different things happening in the music, so you can hear the melody," she continued as I backed out and began to drive away from the school. "And I love Mark Knopfler's voice. His lyrics are so cool."

"True," I said. "They've got one song called 'Private Investigations.' It's like listening to a story."

"How about 'Telegraph Road'?" she asked. "It's one of my favorites."

I realized what was happening. If it kept going, it would be too hard to keep distrusting her. Much as I wanted to like her, I also didn't want to like her.

"You said you had something that you thought I should know even if it hurt me," I said.

It was a quick subject change. I was trying to send a clear message.

"Right," she said, sounding a little hurt. She'd gotten the message.

I was out on the streets now, not sure where I should drive.

"Well then," she said a few seconds later, "it's about your brother."

As if I didn't know.

"Funny you should have mentioned that song by Dire Straits," she continued. "'Private Investigations.'"

I stopped for a red light and glanced over at her. She looked sad.

"You see," she said quietly. "I'm doing a private investigation of my own. And I think your brother is into something criminal."

 # Eighteen

The high school I attended was in the southeast part of the city. Fish Creek Park was nearby, so I drove there and parked. We found a bench to sit on. She set her purse on the table.

"I'll start from the beginning," she said. "My father owns a couple of movie theaters."

"But you drive a beat-up Volkswagen."

She smiled. "Now who is judging who by what they drive?"

"No," I said, "what I meant was that he could probably afford to buy you something better."

"Sure he could. But then it wouldn't be mine, would it?"

She was right, and I liked her for it. So I told myself not to like her. It didn't work.

A few seagulls squawked nearby. They were fighting over half a burger someone had left behind on the grass. Seagulls. Why were they called seagulls when this was the prairies? Or if they really were seagulls, what were they doing here when the nearest sea was so far away?

These weren't questions I would ask out loud. I had other questions for her.

"Does your father own the theater in Kensington?" I asked.

"No," she said. She stared past me and thought for a few seconds. "This is hard to explain. I was in a video store yesterday…"

I coughed.

She raised her eyebrows.

"Just clearing my throat," I said.

She nodded. "This guy sold me an illegal copy of a DVD. He said it would be cheaper than seeing it in a theater, if I shared the cost with my friends…"

"Theater prices *are* pretty high," I said. "Not that I'm agreeing with the guy."

"My dad's business is really suffering. A lot of that is because of piracy."

"Piracy," I said.

"Yeah," Merecedes said. "I'm making a documentary about it."

"Documentary?"

"I want to go to Mount Royal College when

I get out of high school," she said. "They've got a journalism program. The documentary will help me get into the program. And maybe it will help my father too."

I nodded. "Makes sense. And I can understand you wanting to help your dad."

"Piracy is getting bigger and bigger," she said. "Especially in Canada. And now biker gangs are discovering they can make a lot of money from it."

Bikers!

I was beginning to get that horrible feeling in my stomach. She wasn't part of what Nate was doing. She was trying to fight it. And if Nate was part of it, and if it involved bikers…

"Early in the summer, my dad heard a rumor that one of our projectionists was copying movies onto a flash drive. I decided to watch and see what happened."

Mercedes hesitated.

I decided to help her. "And it led you to Nate."

Her eyes widened in surprise.

"You know?"

"Only a little," I said.

"He picked up the flash drive. I didn't know who he was. I just remembered his face. Then I saw his photo in the paper once. So then I knew his name. But it wouldn't do much good to just stop someone like Nate. I wanted to find out who he was working for and how he was getting the illegal copies out of the theaters."

I told her about seeing the guy go into the washroom the same time as Nate. Then I had a question.

"You were at the Hitmen golf tournament to meet him, weren't you?"

"Yes," she said.

"Video camera in your purse?" I asked.

"You know?"

"Don't get mad at me," I said, "but remember a guy with goofy hair and a lame mustache in the video store? That was me."

"You!"

I told her everything. About listening to her conversation with the guy behind the counter. About how his tattoos matched the bikers' tattoos. I told her about the bikers who put me on the train track. The only thing I didn't tell her was the part where the guy in the video store made the rude noise.

As she listened, her face became more and more serious.

"So," I finished, "it turns out you didn't have to worry about telling me something I wouldn't want to hear."

She shook her head sadly.

"Nolan," she said, "how do you think I found

your car at the high school?"

"I had wondered about that," I said.

"It's because I saw you park down the street the night that Nate went to the video store to deliver the flash drive with the pirated movie. Nate saw you too."

"What?"

She pointed to her purse. "You already know I videotaped him in the video store for my documentary. What you don't know is that the first thing he did was make a call on his cell phone."

"That doesn't mean anything," I said.

"Maybe not. But when he came back out, I told him that two bikers had dragged you away from your car."

"What?" Nate had known but hadn't stepped in to help?

"He told me not to worry," she said. "He told me that whatever happened was going to help you and not hurt you." She paused. "That's when I knew he'd been the one to tell those bikers where you were."

 # Nineteen

I stood along the boards in my skates and full equipment and practice jersey. I leaned on my knees, panting. Sweat poured down my face and neck.

Coach Jon had worked us hard in the first hour of practice, mainly with skating drills.

Now it was time for scrimmage.

Coach Jon skated toward me. He carried a yellow practice jersey.

He stopped in front of me. He spoke slowly so that I could read his lips. In practice he wasn't so worried that I would misunderstand him. He saved the whiteboard for games.

"Time to switch teams," I saw him say.

"Switch teams?" I repeated. Maybe I had read his lips wrong. "Am I being traded from the Hitmen?"

"Not yet," he said. "Switch scrimmage teams."

I wore black in practice. We always played against the yellow.

I looked over to see if Nate was wearing a yellow jersey.

Coach Jon caught me looking. He knew why.

"Radar," he said, "you're not on Nate's line anymore."

"Sir?" I said.

"I want to keep you both on the Hitmen. Since it's not working for you on the same line, I want to see how you play with others."

I nodded. I felt sick about this. But what could I do?

"And Radar," Coach Jon said, "you're playing center in this scrimmage."

"Center?" Had he just said center? Why was I suddenly playing center? It had been years since I'd played anything but left wing.

"Center." He smiled a tight smile. "Against Nate."

I lined up at center ice in my yellow jersey. Except for a few games when the Hitmen had faced the Warriors the previous season, Nate and I had never played against each other. Even during those Hitmen-Warriors games last season, our lines had not been on the ice at the same time.

Strange as it felt to be playing center, it felt even stranger to look up from where I was digging in to take the face-off and see my own face on the player opposite me.

Nate's eyes were intense. Angry.

I'm sure mine were the same.

Coach Jon dropped the puck to start the scrimmage. Nate lunged forward and slammed his shoulder into mine, knocking me off the puck. He kicked it forward with the tip of his skate blade, and his left winger—his new left winger—swooped in and raced toward the yellow jerseys' blue line.

I spun and followed, with Nate on my heels.

At our blue line, his winger dumped the puck into the boards and chased. After years as a winger, I nearly made the mistake of drifting to the top of the face-off circle on the left side to guard the point. I reminded myself that I was a center.

I headed toward our net.

So did Nate.

In the corner, his new winger fought a yellow-jerseyed defenseman for the puck. I stayed close to Nate, about half a stride back.

I've noticed some centers like tangling with the player they cover in the defensive end. Others pick their times, going in to bodycheck as a pass arrives.

That's what I decided to do. I was angry enough with Nate that if I covered him too closely, we might end up in a fight.

Sure enough, seconds later the puck squirted to Nate. He thought he was clear, and he began to stickhandle before shooting. He should have fired it right away.

His head was down, and I crashed into him hard, knocking him on his butt. I stood over him, glaring.

He slowly got to his feet. A small drop of blood fell from his nose.

"That was brave," he said, his lips clearly moving. "Hitting me from behind like that. Want to try it again? Right now? While I'm ready?"

I knew he wanted to fight.

So did I. It had been over a month of frustration, of not trusting him. Then to find out that he was working with a gang of bikers. And that he'd sent the bikers after me to scare me away.

Yeah, I was angry. Real angry. And so, so ready to throw a punch at him. But I wasn't going to give him the satisfaction of knowing how frustrated I was.

"I'm sorry," I said. I tapped my ear. "I'm your deaf brother. Remember? I can't hear you."

I skated away without looking back.

# Twenty

"I get why you're angry with Nate," Mercedes said.

"I doubt it," I answered.

We were at the Calgary Zoo, off Memorial Drive. The sun was low and deep shadows stretched from the buildings in front of us. In the background was the screeching of monkeys. And the screeching of kids. Hard to tell them apart, I thought.

When I'd called Mercedes an hour after early afternoon practice finished, she had suggested we meet at the zoo to talk. I'd been fine with it. I'd have been fine with meeting her anywhere, even if it meant crawling across broken glass.

"You're angry," she said, "because he betrayed you. When he knew you were following, he sent those bikers after you."

I let a silence hang over us, not sure if I

should tell her the truth.

She put her hand on mine. "I'd be mad too."

Her hand felt good. Still, I moved away from her. She was with me because she wanted to make a documentary. I was with her because of my brother. No sense fooling myself into believing that she liked me.

"Radar?" she said quietly. "What is it?"

Mothers pushing strollers walked toward us. In the background, elephants walked around doing what elephants do. Eating. Drinking. And…well, you know. The one I watched as I looked away from Mercedes could have filled a wheelbarrow. Things like that impress guys. Usually not girls. I kept my admiration to myself.

"Radar?" she repeated.

"He's not betraying me," I said. "He's betraying my parents."

She frowned. "But he told me your parents are…"

"Dead," I said. "Gone. You don't need to tiptoe around it."

She nodded. "How is he betraying them?"

"We grew up outside Vancouver," I said. "Dad was a cop. In grade five, that's all we knew about his job. Later we found out he was an undercover cop."

"Sounds dangerous."

"A few years after he died, we learned he was trying to work his way into a biker gang that was moving drugs throughout the Lower Mainland."

"Really dangerous."

"Yeah," I said flatly. "It killed him. And my mother."

"But Nate said—"

"That a cement truck hit their car?" I asked.

"Yes."

"It did. What he probably didn't tell you was that the driver had a criminal record and was known to be part of the gang that Dad was trying to crack."

"It wasn't an accident!"

"No," I said, "but no one could prove it. The driver was charged with vehicular manslaughter and spent only six months in prison. Back with his friends in no time."

"Oh," she said very quietly.

"You understand now?" I said. "Nate's working for the same kind of losers who killed our parents. That's what hurts me."

"I'm so sorry," she said.

"Not your fault," I said. "His choice."

"I'm sorry for you."

"Don't feel sorry for me," I said.

"I don't feel sorry *for* you. I'm sorry *with* you."

She was looking straight into my eyes. I believed her.

"I called you to tell you I'll help you with your documentary," I said, "but only if you leave Nate out of it."

"He's part of it," she said. "You can't change that."

"Yes, I can," I said. "That's why I want to make you a deal."

"Deal?" she asked.

"I can get you more information," I said. "Use it to nail the people behind this. The people who are using Nate. But you can't use it to nail Nate."

"But if he's part of it, how can exposing this keep Nate out of trouble?"

"Because I'm going to use the information to force Nate to quit before you finish your documentary."

"I see," she said. "Once he knows you can prove what he's doing, you're going to make sure he stops."

"Something like that," I answered.

We had been walking as we talked. Now we were at the tiger cage. The tiger was sleeping. Like it had no cares in the world. Wished I could sleep like that. No worries about hockey. No worries about my brother.

Mercedes interrupted my thoughts. "You're

going to do your best to help Nate. Even after he betrayed you. Even after he betrayed your parents."

"Yes," I said. "No matter what, he's still my brother."

Twenty-One

The next evening, Mercedes and I sat in her Volkswagen near the back of the parking lot of a downtown pizza place where Nate had stopped to buy dinner. We heard him order a pepperoni with extra cheese.

"Cool," she said. "It works."

After practice I had hidden my FM in Nate's Calgary Hitmen backpack. I had a pack just like it, and I knew he took his everywhere. If he found the FM, I could just tell him that I'd accidentally mixed up our backpacks.

At Radio Shack, I'd found electronic components to rig my processor to send signals to a battery-powered speaker that was now on the dash of Mercedes' Volkswagen. The processor had an attachment port on the bottom that made this possible. It meant that we could hear what

99

was going on in the pizza place. Mercedes also had a digital recorder to pick up the conversation for her documentary.

I could still hear Mercedes' voice through the built-in microphones of my processor.

"Cool," I said back to her. But really, it wasn't. I was spying on my brother. About an hour earlier, with the FM already in his backpack, I had heard him make a phone call setting up a meeting at the pizza place. From Nate's end of the conversation, it sounded like the person he was meeting was involved in illegally copying DVD's. That was why I'd phoned Mercedes.

In the pizza place, Nate spoke. We both heard him. "Max, thanks for coming."

"Snuck through the back," a deep male voice answered. "You know we shouldn't be seen together."

"I know," Nate said. "It's about my brother."

"Radar," Max said.

Tiny snakes of electricity raced up and down my spine. I locked eyes with Mercedes. She didn't say anything.

"He's been following me," Nate said. "I think he suspects something. We need to do something about it."

"Not good," Max said. "Not good at all."

In the background, we heard something metal—maybe a knife—drop on the floor. When someone puts a knife in your back, like Nate was doing to me, it isn't nearly as loud. Except for the noise you make when you feel a sudden sharp pain.

"Thing is," Nate said, "I don't want to quit."

"You're good," Max said. "And it seems to be going good."

"So can I tell him?" Nate asked.

"Dangerous," Max said.

"Radar can handle it," Nate said.

"Think he'll want to be part of this?" Max asked.

"I don't want him part of it," Nate said. "I'm not sure he would want to be part of it either. He's knows why our Mom and Dad died and who killed them."

Good thing my hands weren't around Nate's neck. The word *SNAP* came to my mind, I was so angry at him.

"I'm cool with that," Max said. "Tell him what you need to tell him. Just make sure you don't get caught. We need to make sure, one way or another, that he's completely out of this."

"Completely," Nate said. "I'll take care of it right away."

It sounded like a chair's legs scraping the floor. Was Max standing up?

"That's it then, right?" Max said.

"Except for the money," Nate said.

There was a short pause before Max spoke.

"Fifteen hundred dollars," Max said. "A lot of guys wouldn't do what you're doing."

"I'm not a lot of guys," Nate said.

No kidding, I thought. Give up your brother to a biker gang after bikers were the ones who killed your parents?

Then silence. Max was leaving.

I tapped Mercedes' shoulder.

"The back door," I said. "Max came in through the back door. He'll probably leave through the back door. Let's follow him!"

She started the Volkswagen and moved it closer to the back. Sure enough, a big guy in jeans and a leather coat came out. He had long black hair and a beard. He walked straight to a green pickup truck.

"I don't think he saw us," Mercedes said.

I gave her a thumbs-up, and we began to follow.

She did a great job. Judging by the way he drove, it seemed like he had no idea we were following.

Five minutes later, he stopped, parked and got out of his green truck.

At the last place I would have guessed.

A police station.

 # Twenty-Two

We parked down the street from the police station.

"Now what?" I saw Mercedes say.

I shrugged. My cell phone rang. Actually it vibrated.

I looked at the number. It was Nate.

I held the phone over my processor, not against my ear.

"We need to meet!" Nate said.

"Need to meet," I repeated. "Where?"

He named the pizza place we had left only five minutes earlier. But I wanted to make sure he had no idea that I knew where he was.

"You're cutting out," I said into the phone. "Bad signal. Text me, okay?"

I hung up. Thirty seconds later, another short vibration of my cell phone. His text message was simple: *Meet me at Pizza Palace right away.*

I explained everything to Mercedes.

"Not much use spying on a police station," she said.

"I wrote down the license plate number to the truck," I said. "Just in case that helps."

She nodded and drove back toward the pizza place.

Just as we made it to the parking lot, I saw Nate. He was standing in the doorway with the two big bikers who had put me on the train tracks, Tattoo Biker and Bent Nose Biker.

What had Max said to Nate barely ten minutes ago? *Tell him what you need to tell him. Just make sure you don't get caught. We need to make sure, one way or another, that he's completely out of this.*

And what had Nate replied? *Completely. I'll take care of it right away.*

Sure, he'd taken care of it right away. In about as much time as it took to call in the bikers and as much time as it took to call and set me up.

Mercedes pointed. She saw the bikers too.

"Keep driving," I said. Had she guessed what I had guessed?

"I hate him," I said to Mercedes.

"He asked you to meet him so that the bikers could really take care of you," she said. So she had guessed.

"Slow down," I said. "Don't get out of range of my FM."

There were plenty of vehicles on the street. She zipped in and parked ahead of a truck that hid us from the pizza place.

That's when we heard one of the bikers growl at Nate. It came through very clearly, although my FM was buried in his backpack. It was the biker with the deep, deep voice.

"Let's go," Tattoo Biker said. "For a ride."

"Where?" Nate asked. "Why?"

"Shut up," we heard Tattoo Biker say through the speaker on Mercedes' dash. "Trust me. You'll find out. And when you do, you won't like it."

They pushed him into a white van.

The one they had used to drive me away from Chinatown.

Twenty-Three

We followed. From downtown, the van went east on Memorial and then turned off onto Zoo Drive. There were a few other cars on Zoo Drive, and it was dark. I doubted the bikers knew we were following them.

We passed the lights of the Calgary Zoo. The day before, I thought I'd had plenty to worry about at the zoo. Now, as we passed by it again, I realized things were much worse.

"You're an idiot," Tattoo Biker was saying to Nate. "You really thought you could fool us by pretending we needed to scare your brother away?"

"Don't know what you're talking about," Nate said. My FM was doing a great job, sending the conversation to my processor. At the same time, the processor sent sound to my spider and to the speaker on the dash. Where Mercedes was also recording it.

"We've got a videotape that proves otherwise," the second biker told him. "You sent your brother into Chinatown the next day to snoop around. He was in disguise, but when you run the tape, you can see him hiding something. He's deaf, right? It was a listening device he hid in there. He left it there when some girl went in to ask questions and buy a pirated DVD. And you know who the girl is? The daughter of a guy who owns a bunch of movie theaters."

"You guys are crazy," Nate said. "I don't know what you're talking about."

"No?" came the question from Bent Nose Biker. "We've had someone watching you since then. Tonight he went into the pizza place and sat in a back booth. Our guy saw you have a meeting with the undercover cop. Explain that, why don't you?"

Undercover cop! That's why the black-bearded guy had gone to the police station. He was a cop! Just like our dad.

"Some guy stopped at my table because he knows I play for the Hitmen," Nate said. "If he's an undercover cop, I'll take your word for it."

"Nice try," Tattoo Biker growled. "If that was just coincidence, want to tell us how your parents died?"

Nate didn't answer.

"Your dad was an undercover cop too," Bent Nose Biker said. "Worked the Lower Mainland near Vancouver. A cop who pretended to join a biker gang to try to nail drug dealers."

Nate still didn't answer. My hands were fists. I was beginning to figure things out.

"Yeah," Tattoo Biker said. "We heard one of the bikers in the Vancouver gang was driving a cement truck one day. You know the rest, don't you?"

"I have nothing to say," Nate said.

"We've put two and two together," Tattoo Biker said. "You're some kid trying to get payback. But guess what—you lost."

I thought back on some of what I'd heard Nate say at the pizza place. *He's been following me…We need to do something about it…So can I tell him.*

I remembered Max's answer. *Tell him what you need to tell him. Just make sure you don't get caught. We need to make sure, one way or another, that he's completely out of this.*

This meant that Nate had called me to meet him at the pizza place because Max had given him permission to let me know what was going on. Nate had not called in the bikers. They'd captured him. And now I knew why.

Nate wasn't betraying me. Or our parents.

He was doing what Mercedes was doing. Trying to find a way to stop the bikers.

And now he was in trouble for it. Because of me.

The white van crossed the Bow River and headed toward Blackfoot Trail.

"You know what happens to guys who mess with us?" Bent Nose Biker said. "They have accidents. And since we've only got a few minutes left, let me explain. Up ahead is a drowning machine. You're going to take a long ride."

Drowning machine?

"About once a year we have to do something like this," Tattoo Biker said. "Everyone always thinks it's an accident."

"Drowning machine," Nate repeated. He probably sounded tough to them. But he was my twin brother. I knew his voice. I knew when he was afraid. Like now.

"The weir across the river," Tattoo Biker said. "We throw you in. It's like a giant whirlpool. Might take a day or two to spit your body out."

"We need to call the cops," I said to Mercedes.

But it was too late. The van was already slowing down and turning into Pearce Estate Park. Where the drowning machine waited for my brother.

 # Twenty-Four

The drowning machine.

I'd been there during a high school science class.

Pearce Estate Park was along the Bow River. It was a wetlands area with a huge fish hatchery. Part of the tour had taken us to the weir, which was a low dam all across the Bow River. Water flowed over it, but it also backed up water that was diverted into an irrigation canal.

There was a project to change the weir to make it safer, because anyone falling over the dam was certain to drown. The water going over the dam dropped and cycled around. It was impossible to get out. That's why there was a big sign by the weir warning people not to get into the river.

The sign was right where the bikers were going to throw him in.

The van's brake lights brightened and then disappeared. The van was parked. We were half a block away, and the van had turned down a quiet street into Pearce Estate Park.

"What do we do?" Mercedes asked. "By the time the police get here, it will be too late."

I heard her voice through the processor on my ear. What I heard more clearly was the audio from my FM in Nate's backpack.

"Hey," Tattoo Biker said. "Is that car following us?"

"Drive past the van," I said to Mercedes.

"What?"

"We need to look like we aren't following them," I said. "We'll park and step outside and hold hands like we're going for a walk."

She drove past the van. Far enough away so the bikers couldn't see our faces.

"Ready to hold hands?" I asked.

She smiled at me. "For a lot longer than you think."

What? Good thing it was dark. I blushed.

We stepped outside. She leaned into me. She stood on her toes and kissed the side of my cheek.

Wow.

Then I got mad at myself. Two bikers were about to throw my brother into the river, and I was thinking about her kiss.

"Just two kids," Tattoo Biker said, his voice still transmitted by my FM in Nate's backpack. "We can relax."

"They'll see us get out of the van," Bent Nose Biker said. "Should we take them out too?"

"No," Tattoo Biker said, "we need the drowning to look like an accident. It will be suspicious if they report an assault on the same night that Nate here goes for a long swim."

"What do we do?" Bent Nose Biker asked.

"There's another place to park," Tattoo Biker said. "We'll drive there."

The van behind us turned around.

The good news was that Mercedes had been recording all the conversations that we overheard, which might help put the bikers in jail. The bad news was that they still had Nate. Seeing them in jail wouldn't mean a thing to me if Nate didn't survive.

The van's headlights disappeared.

"I'm going to the river," I said to Mercedes. "You call the cops. Tell them about the weir and what's happening."

"I hope they believe me," she said.

"Remember the license plate number of the undercover cop? If they don't believe this is important, give the plate number. They'll find a way to get hold of the guy."

"What if it takes too long?" she asked.

"That's where I come in," I said.

I squeezed her hand and turned toward the park. It was dark among the trees. I needed to find a way through that darkness to get to the weir in time.

Twenty-Five

At the bank of the river, I found a hiding spot among some trees. It was about twenty steps to the river. The water rushing over the weir sparkled in the moonlight.

I didn't see the bikers or my brother. It meant either the bikers had already been here, thrown Nate into the water and left. Or that I'd beaten all three of them to this spot.

I told myself that it would have taken longer for the three of them to walk there than it had for me to run there. I didn't want to believe that Nate was already in the water below the weir, his body tumbling round and round in the drowning machine.

Upstream from the weir, framed against the night sky, was downtown Calgary. The lights in the windows of the skyscrapers made a backdrop to the river. Where I was, there wasn't enough light, even with the moon, to see a thing. I kicked around, trying to find a big stick.

I wasn't too worried about making noise. I remembered from my science visit that the rush of the river over the weir made it difficult to hear anything, even If you wereren't deaf. That meant that it would cover my crashing around in the bushes.

I hoped Nate still had his backpack with him. That way, with my FM inside, I'd be able to hear them talking when they got in range. It would warn me when they were about fifty steps away.

It took about a minute to find the perfect stick. The size of a baseball bat.

My plan was to wait until the bikers and Nate had passed me. Their backs would be to me. With the sound of the water over the weir to cover the sound of my footsteps, I'd run up behind them. I'd whack one on the head while he wasn't looking. The other biker would notice, of course. If I were lucky, I'd be able to whack him too. If not, I'd still have the stick. If the second guy tried to keep hold of Nate, I'd be able to smack him. If he let go of Nate, Nate and I would be able to run away. We were smaller and lighter and more athletic. No way any biker would be able to catch us.

There was nothing left to do except wait.

"Did you enjoy the money we gave you?" came Tattoo Biker's voice. "Because you're sure going to pay for it."

"Like pay with your life," Bent Nose Biker added.

In a way, it was weird. For anyone else, the noise of the river would have made it difficult to hear any conversation more than five feet away. But the FM in Nate's backpack was my secret weapon.

"Didn't keep a penny of it," Nate said. "I gave it to a police fund that helps families of cops killed in the line of duty. Nice of you to contribute."

I remembered the conversation I'd heard between Nate and Max in the pizza place. *Fifteen hundred dollars*, Max had said. *A lot of guys wouldn't do what you're doing.*

I'm not a lot of guys, Nate had said.

Nate had been giving the money away. Not keeping it. I felt horrible for believing the worst about Nate.

"You did this just to give away money?" Bent Nose Biker said.

"No," Nate said, "to get enough evidence to help the cops bust you guys, the way my dad was trying to stop bikers. I wasn't going to keep your money. Neither would my dad."

"Any other last words?" Tattoo Biker said. "Not that anyone is going to hear them."

I saw them now. Three dark shapes walking toward the river. There was a small circle of light pointing at the ground. A flashlight.

Nate knew the bikers were taking him to the river to drown him. Why wasn't he trying to run?

"The cops will know the drowning wasn't an accident," I heard Nate say. "They'll hunt you down for this. Enjoy life in prison."

Closer now, I could see why Nate hadn't tried to run. It looked like they had a dog leash around his neck. Tattoo Biker was holding on to the end of the leash. This complicated things.

"What the cops know and what they can prove are two different things," Tattoo Biker said. "Without witnesses, they have nothing. They'll just find your drowned body and your backpack with it. This stun gun won't leave any marks that point to murder. All it does is paralyze you and make it easy to throw you in the water."

Stun gun!

I'd been so worried about the drowning machine, I'd forgotten about the stun gun the bikers had used on me by the train tracks. That's what they were going to do: Make him as helpless as I had been and then throw him in like a sack of potatoes.

How could I stop them now?

Twenty-Six

I stepped out from the trees. I stood between the three of them and the river.

"That's far enough," I said as loudly and as boldly as my fear let me.

The flashlight beam hit my face, blinding me.

"It's his brother!" Bent Nose Biker said.

I turned sideways to take the light directly out of my eyes. It would still let me see if the beam moved closer.

"Do you point at the sky and tell people it's blue?" I said.

"Huh?" Bent Nose Biker answered.

"That's a way of saying that you point out the obvious," I said. "Of course, people dumb enough to point out the obvious do it because they're not smart enough to see the obvious."

"Be just as fun to get rid of both of you," Tattoo

118

Biker said.

"Run," Nate yelled. "Don't let—"

Nate gagged. Tattoo Biker had yanked on the leash.

"Shut up," Tattoo Biker said pleasantly to Nate. "Or you get more of the choke chain."

They'd been dragging my brother along, just like a dog on a choke chain.

Sudden fury filled my head like the roar of an avalanche, a fury that took over my body as if I were a puppet.

My head was down and I was charging forward without even considering what might happen next. I had the stick in my hands like a lance.

The flashlight beam blinded me again.

But I was all right with that. It gave me a target.

I didn't come in swinging. I came in with the stick pointed forward, like a knight charging a dragon.

They'd been dragging my brother along, just like a dog.

I wanted to put the spear through the biker.

I hit something—hard. Heard a scream of pain.

At the same time, something hit me—hard. It felt as if I were on the C-train tracks and the train had actually smashed into me. I knew what it was. I'd been popped with the stun gun as I hit the biker who held the flashlight. The burst of electric shock sent every nerve ending of my body into a spasm, and my legs buckled.

On the C-train tracks, I'd been standing still when the electric prod hit me. Here, I'd been moving fast. As I lost control over all my muscles, I tumbled forward like a rag doll.

I saw a rolling circle of light. The stun gun flashlight. I couldn't do anything. Not even reach for it.

But another hand did.

Just like on the C-train tracks, I could see and think. What I couldn't do was move. I recognized the hand as Nate's. Then his hand and the flashlight disappeared as he was jerked out of my sight by the biker holding the choke chain.

This is it, I thought.

I can't move. They'll drag me to the river. They'll shock Nate and drag him to the river too.

I heard a scream from Nate's direction.

Something thumped me. A boot. The biker that I'd knocked to the ground was up again and had just kicked me. I braced myself for another kick.

Instead I heard a second scream. From the biker.

What was happening?

I found out a second later as someone knelt in front of me. Two hands grabbed my shoulder and lifted me. In the moonlight, I saw silver glinting from what looked like a giant necklace.

"Nate?" I managed to say. It wasn't a necklace. It was the choke chain.

"'You point at the sky and tell people it's blue'?" he said. "Of course it's me."

I was shaking. He pulled me close and hugged me.

"I don't get it," I said. My voice was croaky, but I was starting to get some control of my muscles. "I thought he got you with the prod too."

"Nope," Nate said. "Look."

He turned the flashlight beam toward the bikers. Both were on the ground, curled up like worms.

"This flashlight stun gun is wicked," he said. "You knocked it from his hand when you charged him. I fell and grabbed it. When the guy yanked me in again, I gave him a good shot. Then a shot to the guy kicking you."

Both bikers were starting to get to their knees.

"Hang on," Nate said. "Hate to say it, but I'm going to enjoy this."

He took a couple of steps. Jabbed one with the stun gun and then the other.

Both screamed and toppled again. Nate slipped the choke chain off his neck and dropped it over Tattoo Biker's neck.

"Hate to say it," I said, "but I enjoyed that too."

Nate tilted his head instead of answering me. He had heard it first.

Then I heard it, filtered through the FM in his backpack. And from my processor. The *thump-thump* sound of a helicopter.

Seconds later a floodlight hit us. I knew what it was. I guess I had just as much to explain to Nate as he did to me. I was very glad we were going to have time to do the explaining.

"Friends in high places!" I yelled at Nate. Mercedes had gotten through to someone. "Police chopper."

Twenty-Seven

We were down three goals, halfway into the third period against Vancouver, when Coach Jon finally gave Nate and me some ice time by sending us out for a face-off on the left side of the ice in our end.

Although I felt like a spring colt that had been trapped in a stall for two days, I managed not to kick up my heels and gallop as I jumped out of the players' box. I took my spot just in front of Rooster and in front of our goalie.

I felt good for a few reasons. The first was that Nate and I were talking again. He had told me that the cash he had at the charity golf tournament was money that he was going to donate. Just like he was going to donate the winnings of his little golf trick, after explaining it to the people who'd made wagers. His new clothes were so he would look like someone who wanted money enough to get involved with bikers. He'd been trying to protect me by keeping everything a secret. He'd even called the bikers and asked them to scare me, to make it look like I wasn't part of it. Of course, he thought they were only going to threaten me, not put me on train tracks.

The second reason I felt good was because Mercedes had agreed to go out with me again, on a real date. I would get to see more of that smile. Lots more.

I also felt good because of this—the chance to play.

When the puck dropped, it was my job to head toward the point, in case Nate lost the draw.

He didn't.

But he didn't win either.

He and the Vancouver center fought for the puck between their skates. I stepped in and jabbed it loose. Somehow I knew that Nate would squirt free and chase it. So I spun off for some open ice.

Before the puck reached my stick, I knew it was coming, even with my back to it. Don't ask how. I just knew that Nate knew where I was headed and that he would slap it toward me.

I widened my legs slightly.

Sure enough, the puck came through. Softly.

Like a butterfly waiting to land on my stick.

I had plenty of energy. I kicked it up a gear and raced over our blue line into the neutral zone, puck on my stick. Their defenseman made an aggressive move to check me.

I dropped the puck for Nate.

A lot of young players think that a drop pass needs to be pushed backward. Wrong. The best thing to do is stop the puck and keep skating forward. That way your teammate doesn't have to try to juggle a puck coming toward him. Instead it's waiting like a ripe cherry.

I left my drop pass in place but skated hard toward the Vancouver defenseman. I bounced off him, but because he had been making the move toward me, there wasn't an interference call.

Quick glance behind me. Nate had swooped on the puck and gone wide. I drifted a little toward center ice. I wanted to give him an outlet if he needed it. He did.

The other defenseman cut him off. Nate shoveled the puck back. As soon as it hit the tape on my stick, I flicked it back to him. A classic give-and-go.

Nate got the puck at their blue line. Clear ice between him and the net.

I tangled briefly with the Vancouver center but had plenty of steam to beat him in a race to their net.

I was skating at top speed. No chance to catch Nate. He was in full stride too. My job now was to get ready for a rebound.

Good thing I was watching so closely.

Nate pulled the goalie with a great move to his backhand. With the wide-open net, Nate did something I'd never seen before. He passed it back to me.

Even though I was watching so closely, even though our radar system seemed to be working again, it still surprised me.

I almost missed his pass.

I caught it with my stick, bobbled it briefly; then I kept my knees low and fired a screamer into the upper right side of the net.

I raised my hands in the air!

Nate caught up to me as I circled.

"It's the new me," he said. No one else would have been able to hear him above the noise of the crowd. I didn't need to. I saw his face clearly. Not only how his lips moved. But that he meant it. "From here on, brother, it's going to be more equal."

I grinned back. High-fived him.

We scored another goal that shift.

Two more by the time the game ended. With a victory for the Hitmen.

It was great to have my brother back.

READ ON!
LITERACY PROJECT

On behalf of ReadOn! Literacy, I want to congratulate the employees of Schlumberger, the Calgary Hitmen, coolreading.com, Sigmund Brouwer, and a host of volunteers for their contributions to the Literacy for Life Program. Their outstanding support has made the program tremendously successful again this year. 'Hats-off' to Schlumberger for adding outstanding role models like Hall-of-Famer Bryan Trottier and other NHL stars such as Philadelphia's Al Conroy and Calgary Flames' Paul Kruse to the program. Their involvement means even more young people will be impacted in communities throughout this country.

This year's campaign has once again seen thousands of books placed into the hands of students free of charge. Speaking of students, we would love to hear from you. Please drop us a line at literacyforlife@shaw.ca to let us know how you have enjoyed this year's novel and why you think reading is important. Just for giving us some feedback you could win some great prizes for yourself and your school. We're giving away author visits from Sigmund Brouwer, visits from Calgary Hitmen players, tickets for your class to attend a game, and all kinds of collectible Calgary Hitmen prizes. We look forward to hearing from you and encourage your participation in the program. We hope you have enjoyed the book as much as we have enjoyed bringing it to you! See you at a Hitmen Game!

Take good care,
John McMullen, Chairman
ReadOn! Literacy

Students, ..Please send your responses to
literacyforlife@shaw.ca,
or mail to: ReadOn! Literacy Project,
45 William Bell Drive, Leduc, AB, T9E 6N1